Arms Dealers

CLAW & WARDER

Episode 2

ERIK HENRY VICK

RATATOSKR PUBLISHING

NEW YORK

RATATOSKR PUBLISHING
2080 NINE MILE POINT ROAD, UNIT 106
PENFIELD, NY 14526

PUBLISHER'S NOTE: THIS IS A WORK OF FICTION. NAMES, CHARACTERS, PLACES, AND INCIDENTS ARE A PRODUCT OF THE AUTHOR'S IMAGINATION. LOCALES AND PUBLIC NAMES ARE SOMETIMES USED FOR ATMOSPHERIC PURPOSES. ANY RESEMBLANCE TO ACTUAL PEOPLE, LIVING OR DEAD, OR TO BUSINESSES, COMPANIES, EVENTS, INSTITUTIONS, OR LOCALES IS COMPLETELY COINCIDENTAL.

ARMS DEALERS/ ERIK HENRY VICK. -- 1ST ED.
ISBN 978-1-951509-05-7

TABLE OF

CONTENTS

For all of you who risked your own health providing essential services for everyone else during the COVID-19 pandemic.

I hope you enjoy *Arms Dealers*. If so, please consider joining my Readers Group—details can be found at the end of the last chapter.

CHAPTER I

THE BODY

In the Locus of New York, crimes committed by magical entities threaten the delicate balance between the mundane world and the supernatural realm.

The dedicated teams of detectives who investigate these breaches of Canon and Covenants are members of an elite unit known as the Supernatural Inquisitors Squad.

These are their stories.

I

Katy Costello checked her watch for the fourth time. Her bestie, Michelle Williams, was late...*again.* Katy stomped her foot in frustration and glanced up and down the block, but she still saw no sign of her friend, and the movie was about to start.

She swiped away the lock screen on her phone, and her thumb hovered over the texting app for a moment. *I've* already *texted her three times. Time to get medieval on her ass.*

With a little grin at her internal comedian, she tapped Michelle's contact and dialed her number. It rang and rang until Katy became convinced that it would go to voicemail, but at the last second, someone picked up. Heavy breathing sounds filled her ear, and Katy grimaced.

"If you're standing me up to get laid *again*, Michelle, I'm going to kick your ass, girlfriend."

Something—or *someone*—choked for breath on the other end, and, following two meaty thunks that came within a split-second of each other, the choking escalated into a sort of moaning.

"Michelle?" Katy's heart leaped and thrashed against her ribs. "Michelle? Are you okay?" A squawk that sounded like it came from a wounded pigeon flew across the line. "Michelle!" Katy cried. "Michelle! Where are you?"

A rattling thump followed by the sound of fingers scrabbling on concrete came next.

"Michelle!"

"Who's dis?" asked a male voice with a serious case of raspy throat.

"Put Michelle on!"

"Nunh. Girl's hurt."

"My God! What's wrong with her?"

"Car."

"Car what? She was hit by a car?"

"Yellow Cab."

"What's that mean? Was she hit by a cab? Where are you?"

"Unnh. Alley off West 71st Street and West End. You come. Unh?"

"How'd she get hit by a cab in an alley? Who the hell are you?"

"Drive da cab. Girl hurts."

Great, thought Katy. *Michelle's hurt, and the only person who'd help her is a cabbie who can't speak English. I hate this city.*

"You...unnnh...you come?"

"Yeah, buddy. Keep your shirt on, I'm coming. I'm three or four blocks away, so it'll take me a few minutes. Stay with her, okay? You stay with her."

"Unh. I wait for you. Hurry."

"Stay on the line in case I—" The line went dead. Katy thought about calling back but dismissed the idea. She could always do that later if she couldn't find them, and the idea of running with her phone pressed to her ear seemed like torture.

She turned away from the Lincoln Square movie theater and sprinted across Broadway, then kept running down the sidewalk of 68th Street. She planned on saving a bit of time by cutting through the green area behind the synagogue on Amsterdam, then trucking up West End Avenue. The only alleys she could think of were around the building on the northeast side of the intersection between West 71st Street and West End.

She sprinted across Amsterdam, ignoring the furious screech of tires and cacophony of horns, and plunged down the tree-lined alley to the north of the synagogue. She hooked a left around the playground, then angled across 70th, hitting the sidewalk a quarter of a block from West End.

She stretched out her stride, ignoring the stares of the people strolling on the sidewalk, and leaned into the turn, almost crashing into a mother pushing a stroller. She didn't stop; she poured on even more speed as she passed the bus stop. Katy raced across the 71st Street crosswalk without looking for traffic, but then she faltered and slowed.

There were no cabs in sight, yellow or otherwise. Half a block later, she turned into the alley and slowed to a cautious walk. "Hello?" she called. The alley was dark and forbidding, and Katy slowed further. "Hello?"

She turned on the flashlight app on her phone and flipped the screen away from her, holding it up. The alley was a narrow one, barely wide enough for a person to walk without turning sideways, but it was empty.

"Dammit," she muttered, jogging to the end of the alley. She peered south at the corner but could see no one in the alley. She turned off the flashlight app and redialed Michelle's phone.

It rang somewhere to the south, and she followed the sound into the alley running behind the building, which, if memory served her, was shaped like a giant backward F. *Probably in the courtyard, if it can be called that. But why isn't that damn cabbie answering the phone again?*

Katy increased her pace, rounding the corner to the courtyard at a dead run, Michelle's phone ringing and ringing from the darkness ahead. "Michelle!" she called. "Cabbie guy!"

No one answered her, but she thought she heard a faint, shuffling step back behind the dumpsters deep in the courtyard. She ran to the end of the courtyard, then skidded to a stop.

"Oh my God! Michelle!" she cried. She wanted to go to her friend, to try and help, but the gruesome scene held her frozen. *How can there be that much blood?*

Michelle's body made an island in a red sea, but there was something off…something Katy didn't—couldn't—get her mind wrapped around. She cocked her head to the side. "Michelle?" she murmured.

"Thanks for coming, unnh," said that gruff-voiced cabbie from somewhere behind her.

Katy glanced over her shoulder, prepared to fight for her life—to claw, to bite, to gouge out his eyes—but when she saw the cabbie, her brain turned off completely, and the courtyard echoed with her scream.

She only had time for one.

2

Leery Oriscoe bumped his car up onto the sidewalk in front of 246 West End Avenue, bleary-eyed and already exhausted. He got out, grimacing at the cold wind that raced past him, and twitched up the collar of his camel hair coat. He squinted at the cop standing post at the end of the alley beside the building. "Laurell? Is that you?"

"Yeah, Oriscoe. You going blind in your old age or what?"

"Yeah, yeah. Who'd you piss off to get this assignment?"

Corporal Laurell Hamilton smiled at him and hooked her thumb at the alley behind her. "Your partner's already down there. Go to the end of the alley, hook a right, then again when you come to the courtyard. Your bodies are down at the end."

"Bodies *plural*, Hamilton?"

She nodded, solemn-faced. "Two of 'em. Or what's left of two of 'em."

"Right. This gets better and better." Leery grunted and hunched his shoulders to protect his neck from the bastard wind. "Hey, you want to switch jobs, Hamilton?"

"Nah. I like my job. It gives me plenty of time to think about writing a book or two."

"You sure? Think of the glory."

Hamilton laughed and shook her head. "No thanks, Oriscoe. I'll stick right where I am."

"Hey, an attitude like that could get you stuck in the urban sprawl forever, Hamilton."

She grinned. "I'll take my chances."

3

Dru stood at the edge of a wide pool of blood, silhouetted by the bright lights ringing the crime scene, staring down at the bodies lying at its center. She had her hands in her pockets, but a *venti* coffee sat atop one of the dumpsters.

Leery smiled and picked up the cup. "Good morning, Princess. Thanks for the joe, but next time, splurge for a *trenta.*"

"Don't call me that," murmured Dru with a distracted air.

"What do we have?" Leery stepped up beside her and stared down at the scene. "Jeez. Someone give these two a hand."

"Hardy-har," said Dru. "What do you think? Cannibals? Werewolves?" She peeked at him from the corner of her eye.

Payback for the princess comment, Leery thought. "Nah. They left too much meat on the bone for wolves. Cannibals? Maybe the mundane variety of psycho. Besides, by comparative mass, the arms are two of the worst things to take for meat."

Dru grunted and held out her hand toward the two armless corpses. "Then what?"

"Maybe the killer couldn't figure out those damn clasps on their bracelets. Only lunatics can work those damn things."

"And women."

"That's what I said, isn't it?" Leery turned and gazed at the blood splatter coating the walls of the narrow courtyard. "Looks like there was more than one perp."

"How can you tell that?"

Leery waved his *venti* at the wall on the left. "Look at the spray patterns. See how they are almost symmetrical? That means the arms came off at the same time."

"How do you figure that?"

"I don't know about you, but if someone hacks off one of my arms, I'm going to turn and run. So, say that happens, and the guy hacks off my other arm... Where does the blood go?"

"Oh, right. The same wall. But would you turn and run *deeper* into the dead-end courtyard to try to get away?"

Leery squatted on his haunches and waved his coffee cup at the bodies. "Look again, Nogan. Tell me what you see."

"Two women, face down in a pool of blood."

"Right."

"And?"

"They're *face down*, Dru, heads toward the dead-end." He peered up at her.

"So...they were both facing the dead-end, and someone hit them from behind?"

"Bingo. What else do you see?"

"Uh..."

"Cell phones, Nogan."

Her eyes zipped to the pair of phones lying at the edge of the shadows toward the end of the courtyard. "Maybe they tried to phone for help."

"This was an ambush." Leery jerked his chin at the body closest to them. "This was the second victim. The perp used the body of the first woman as bait. Probably talked to the second vic on the phone—probably told her that her girlfriend was hurt and gave her directions."

"You see all that from a pair of cellphones and some blood splatter?"

"My mother always said I was gifted."

"Your mother was a smartass, too?"

"Didn't I tell you she was devout catholic that married a Black Hat? Of course she was a smartass." He stood with a groan.

"Starting to show your age, Leery?" asked Nogan with a little smirk.

"Nah. Let's just say this call interrupted some vigorous exercise."

"Eww. TMI, Leery. TMI."

"Hey, you asked."

"Are you at least being safe? Using protection?"

Leery loosened his collar and fished an amulet out. "Never leave home without it, Dru. I still owe you for this, by the way."

"It's my job."

Leery cocked an eyebrow at her.

"Even if you use it for extracurricular, uh, exercise with one of my mother's kind."

"Your kind, too, right?" Leery looked back at the bodies arrayed before them. "We better call the spooks."

"Your partner already did."

Leery turned and watched the woman walk out of the shadows and into the circle cast by the work lights. "Oh. It's you."

The woman was thin and had delicate features, though Leery knew all that was a lie. She spared a moment's glance at Dru before smirking at him. "Aren't you dead yet, Oriscoe?"

"Hey, look, Dru. It's a real live spook."

"Where's your flea collar, Cujo?"

"The same place as your size sixty shoes. Dru, I'd like you to meet my, uh, *friend*, Jenn DuBrava Hinton."

"Friend? *Friend*? Oh, you really know how to hurt a girl, Leery."

"Fine. Dru, meet my nemesis. Don't step closer though, she has feet the size of school buses." Leery waved his coffee cup at Hinton. "And don't mind how she looks. She's got a lot in common with your mother. Except for the big feet and the whole seductress thing."

Dru arched one eyebrow.

Hinton turned her gaze on Dru. "You don't look like one blessed."

"Illusions are useful tools, aren't they?"

Hinton winked at her. "You don't know the half of it."

"Dru's my Warder, Hinton."

"Really, Leery? I'd *never* have guessed."

"Are all demons sarcastic or is it just you two?"

Dru and Jenn exchanged a glance and then chuckled. "You don't know the meaning of sarcasm until you've spent a day or two in Hell," said Jenn.

4

Leery strolled back down the alley with a fresh cup of java in each paw. He put one of the cups down on top of a convenient dumpster.

Dru glanced over and shook her head. "No thanks, Leery. I'm not in the mood for coffee."

"Good, because that would have been awkward. They're both for me."

"How can you drink that much coffee every day?"

"How can I not?"

Dru raised an eyebrow and pursed her lips. "Where do you put it all?"

"I store it in my werewolf half. That way I never need to pi—"

"I get it."

"Hey, can you two get a room or something? Something that involves shutting the hell up?" Leery glanced down the courtyard to where Hinton stood inside a pentagram chalked onto the concrete. Black candles burned at the five points of the star, and each candle's flame was a different color.

The delicate, thin woman was gone, and in her place stood a tall hunch-backed demon with enormous feet. Maroon scales the color of dried blood covered her, and two smaller horns flanked a larger one growing from the center of her forehead. Her eyes glowed purple, and her tail thrashed back and forth.

"Uh-oh," said Leery. "Mommy's mad." He raised his giant cup of coffee to his lips and took a long swig while Jenn glared at them through narrowed eyes. "Hey, I didn't slurp it."

Jenn rolled her eyes and turned back toward the crime scene. She began chanting in *Verba Patiendi*, the sound of her voice doubling, then trebling, and doubling yet again, until Leery's ears rang with discord. Dru stood listening with a faint smile on her lips.

"You like that gobbledygook?"

She glanced at him, and her smile faded. "It's my first language. Mother didn't speak French, so father learned the Language of Suffering."

Leery rolled his shoulders. "Nice. I don't think my parents even knew there was another language besides Bronxian."

"Bronxian?"

"Yeah, da real language of suffering," he said, putting on a heavy Bronx accent. "Except for Hebrew and Yiddish, of course, but in my neighborhood, that was par for the course. I knew more Yiddish as a toddler than English, although I thought it was *all* English."

"Hmm," said Dru, turning her attention back to Hinton's invocation.

The air above the bodies began to shimmer and shift as though populated by heat-devils from the high desert. Wind began to circle in the tight confines of the courtyard, hurling paper and other refuse into a tornado of garbage that stabbed toward the sky.

"I hate this part," Leery grumbled.

"Shh," said Dru.

The shimmering air began to coalesce into the glowing forms of two women whose faces matched the bodies lying on the concrete beneath them. One of the spirits looked past Hinton, and her gaze settled on Leery as though she could command him. The other looked down and started screaming.

"Relax!" snapped Hinton. "Don't tell me you didn't already know you were dead. I know you did, so drop the histrionics."

The screams cut off, and the spirit looked abashed. "What—"

The other spirit barked a laugh. "Shut up, Michelle. Because of you, I'm dead."

"I'm sorry," said Michelle in the voice of a small child.

"Benji? You want to ask the questions?" Hinton called over her shoulder.

"Why not?" Leery walked to stand behind Hinton, careful not to disturb the chalk drawing she stood in. "Ladies, I'm Leery Oriscoe. I'm an NYPD detective. Part of a special unit called the Supernatural Inquisitors Squad. Someone will tell you more about that in your indoctrination, so don't worry about it for now."

"You're going to catch that...that...*whatever* it was?"

"Yeah. Can you describe them?"

"Them? There was only one. A huge monstrosity with what looked like tree bark for skin."

Leery nodded to himself. "Norwegian Wood Troll. Nasty brutes. But are you sure there weren't two of them?"

"No, only one. Why would you think otherwise?"

He waved one of his cups of coffee at Katy's armless body. "Both your arms fell off at about the same time, right?"

"Yeah. He had an ax in each hand. He swung like this." She mimicked two over-hand chops perpendicular to the ground. "Both hit at the same time, and then...and then..."

"Don't worry about it," said Leery. "It'll be hazy for a while."

She treated him to a single nod.

"Okay, so one Norwegian Wood Troll, but two axes?"

"Yes."

"And that's all?"

"No, there was another one, too," said Michelle in her childish voice. "An ugly little guy with a beautiful voice."

"Oh?" Leery arched an eyebrow at her, and when she returned his stare with empty eyes, he shrugged. "Okay, we'll get back to him. The big one, what did he do with them?"

"After he chopped off my arms? He slid the axes into his belt."

"Not the axes. Your arms."

Katy closed her eyes and seemed to grow more translucent. Jenn murmured something singsong in the *Verba Patiendi,* and the spirit's image solidified again. The ghost opened her mouth as though to suck in a deep breath, and her eyes snapped open as nothing happened.

"No lungs," said Leery. "You'll get used to that, too."

The spirit shuddered but otherwise held it together. "Right. He stuffed my arms into this big sack he carried. It was like leather but had clumps of hair all over it."

"Trolls don't make the best tanners." Leery gestured at Michelle. "Is that what he did with your arms, too?"

Michelle glanced at him wide-eyed, then turned away and began humming a nursery rhyme set to music.

"Yeah," said Katy. "It looked like the bag was heavy with...with..."

"Right. Anything you remember about the troll? Any distinguishing features?"

"You mean other than being a troll? I really didn't notice."

"How big was he?"

"I don't know. Maybe half again as big as you."

"So, nine or ten feet. That makes sense." He nodded his head toward Michelle. "Did she tell you how she ended up back here?"

Katy grimaced. "All she said was she 'followed the song.'"

"Followed the song, eh?"

"Yeah. Does that mean something to you?"

Leery took another gulp of coffee. "Sure does. Anything else you can tell me?"

"It happened so fast..."

"Yeah, it always does." Leery glanced at Hinton and nodded. She uttered a phrase in the Language of Suffering and both spirits faded away.

"Want me to check for unseelie activity?" she asked.

"Yes."

Nodding, Hinton closed maroon lids over her glowing purple eyes and chanted softly. The air began to shimmer as it had when she conjured the dead women, but this time it created a glowing river in midair. The river went from behind one of the dumpsters, out of the courtyard, and then turned right into the alley. "Definitely a bugge," murmured Hinton.

"Well, there goes my relaxing weekend off," Leery grumbled.

"Why would an unseelie and a wood troll act in concert?" asked Dru.

"Normally, they wouldn't," said Hinton, letting her invocation fade.

"You can bet there's a motivating force behind it all."

"What kind of motivation would bring a troll and an unseelie together?"

"The same kind that makes politicians from either side of the aisle work in concert: money. It's a great equalizer."

5

Lieutenant Van Helsing appeared next to Leery's desk as he and Dru came in. "What's the story, Oriscoe?"

Dru jumped and rolled her eyes.

"Oh, hey there, Lieu. Don't mind my partner here, she just met Hinton. She's still *spooked*."

"Have you ever considered a career in comedy, Leery?"

"Sure, that's why I joined the NYPD."

"Oh, he's got jokes, now," said Van Helsing in a dead voice.

"Yeah, uh, so, the bodies near West End."

"*If* you have the time," said Epatha.

"Right. Two women. Both bled to death following the amputation of both arms. Michelle Williams and Katy Costello. Both residents of Lincoln Square. We guessed—"

"Their *arms*?"

"Yeah, Lieu. Both arms are missing from each corpse, and that's the only thing missing. Both women have their jewelry, their wallets and ID, even their phones."

"Tell me why it's our case."

Leery glanced at Dru and gave her a slight shake of his head, warning her off. "We figured it was an ambush of the second victim. The first seems to have been pure misfortune on the victim's part—she was unfortunate enough to be caught in an unseelie's summoning song—but the second...that was a crime of opportunity. Hinton's preliminary invocations back that up."

"Suspects?"

"Uh, everyone southwest of 220th street."

"Why exclude the Bronx?" snapped Van Helsing."

"Because you'd think I'm a smartass if I included them," said Leery with a wry grin.

"Yeah, right." Van Helsing rolled her eyes, but she couldn't hide the beginnings of a grin.

"We think a Norwegian Wood Troll did the heavy lifting, and, of course, an unseelie to sing the summoning song."

"That pairing seems unlikely."

"Sure, but that's what the victims told us when Hinton summoned them."

"What other evidence is there?"

Leery shrugged. "Not much. The wounds look weird, but until Liz does her thing, we won't know much else."

"We have the phones," said Dru.

"Oh, right. The way I figure it, Lieu, the first vic was in the wrong place, yaddy. The perp answered an incoming call from the second victim and laid on some story about her friend being hurt."

"Like you said, ambush."

"And they say you're losing touch with the street."

"Who says that?" said Epatha, turning a freezing gaze on Oriscoe.

Leery shrugged out of his coat and pretended he didn't hear her. "Anyway, both vics took simultaneous blows at the shoulders, and it looks like both arms came off with a single strike."

"That takes strength."

"And precision."

Epatha looked at him. "But working with an unseelie?"

"Who else could do it, Lieu? That kind of strength..."

"And that precision would come from centuries of melee violence."

"Right."

"But that's blocks and blocks from the Queensboro Bridge. That's the closest one, right?"

Leery shrugged. "Hey, this is the modern era, Lieu. Even trolls have driver's licenses these days."

"Yeah, but I've never heard of a troll doing something like this."

Van Helsing arched an eyebrow at her.

"Uh, away from a bridge, I mean."

"Hey, even trolls can find gainful employment in the age of Craig's List."

"Hitmen?"

Van Helsing shook her head. "Mercenaries." The lieu floated aimlessly away from their desks. She turned back and looked at Leery. "What kind of asshole would want to send this kind of message?"

Leery shrugged. "It's worse than that, Lieu. The victims were mundanes."

"Oh, great. A troll and an unseelie teamed up to commit murder, and they didn't even have the good grace to kill a supernatural? Now I'll have the Mayor and his grace, the Cynosure, breathing down my neck by way of the Locus Magister, the Chief of Ds, and everyone else."

"Too bad we can't pick the victims of the crimes we investigate."

"Yeah, too bad," said Epatha as she began to fade in and out. She disappeared without another word.

"Is she..."

"Yeah, she's gone, Dru."

"She's so uptight."

"You try being the daughter of a famous paladin turned Grand Cynosure, then dying in the line of duty and coming back to work the next day. It's enough to make anyone cranky."

CHAPTER 2

THE
INVESTIGATION

I

Leery turned into an alley between East 60th and East 59th and pulled bumper to bumper with a silver Chrysler minivan. Dru rolled her head to look at him as he goosed the go pedal and the rear tires began to shriek and smoke.

"You could always find an open spot."

"What, and miss all this fun?" Leery turned a smile on her. "Anyway, you women really go in for a bad boy in a car."

"Not once we turn fourteen." She rolled her eyes and turned her gaze away.

Hopping and skidding in the gutter, the minivan slid until it ground against a dumpster in the shade of the Ed Koch Queensboro Bridge. With a self-satisfied smile, Leery put the car in park. "See there? That's a ten-out-of-ten parking job right there."

"Right." Dru pulled the door lever and slid out of the Crown Vic. "Why are we here?" Her gaze traversed the white, dome-like covering of the tennis club that reminded her of a giant marshmallow, then she twisted to face the commercial building opposite it. "None of this looks residential."

"That whole lives-under-a-bridge thing is a misconception. The actual Covenant dictates that they live under *the shadow* of a bridge."

Dru spun and scanned the tall apartment buildings lining either side of the bridge. "*They*? Trolls? I certainly hope you have more to go on than that. It could take us a lifetime to canvas all of this."

"Don't worry, Nogan. I've got a plan." Leery started walking toward 1st Avenue and Dru followed, shaking her head.

"Want to let me in on it?"

"What, I should ruin the surprise?"

"Yes."

"Fine, Nogan. Fine. Stage one of the plan is I walk down here to the corner. You can come if you want."

"And what will you do at the corner?"

Leery glanced at her, quirked a shaggy eyebrow, and grinned. "Grab a cup of java. Starbucks, there's one on every corner."

Dru stopped walking. "*More* coffee?"

Leery turned to face her, his grin widening. "Hey, you don't look this good without making sacrifices, Nogan. Coffee is the manna of the gods."

"No god I know, and I know a few." Dru shrugged. "Come on, Leery. We don't have time for this."

"There's always time for a Starbucks, Nogan. Besides, I think you'll like the barista."

Dru allowed a sigh to hiss between her teeth. "And why is that?"

Oriscoe's eyes twinkled, and he tipped her a wink. "Oh, you'll have to come along to find out."

"Fine," she said.

"Fine." Leery turned and strolled around the corner, gazing at the trees planted in their clever little boxes of earth.

Dru followed a step behind and couldn't help but smile at his back. Their little arguments had become a thing she looked forward to, and she thought he felt the same. "Oh, look, Oriscoe. A bus lane. You could have parked right out front."

"Two things, Nogan. First, that would be illegal. Second, I didn't want Einar to spot us coming." He grabbed the outer door of the Starbucks and grinned at her.

"Einar?"

"You'll see."

Dru stepped through the door Leery held open for her. When she glanced behind the counter, she froze in mid-stride for a split second, then had to shuffle forward to keep from tripping. "I suppose it's too much to ask that you pretend you didn't see me do that?"

"Relax, Nogan. Almost everyone does that when they see their first troll up close and personal."

2

Leery slapped his hand on the stainless-steel counter in the back room of the Starbucks. "Come on, Einar! Don't you dare hold back on me."

The enormous man blew out a breath, rolled his eyes at Dru, and pushed back out into the front of the shop. He stood at least seven foot four inches tall and had dark mahogany-toned skin, weathered and leathery. He returned a moment later, ducking his head to clear the door frame, with a larger cup of coffee. He carried muscles on top of his muscles and was what Leery's mother called "big-boned." "There. I assume one *trenta* is enough?"

Leery took the cup from Einar's hand. "For now, Einar. For now."

"Unnh. Oriscoe, I got to get back to work."

"Not so fast, big and ugly. We've got questions, and you'd better have answers."

Einar straightened his back, his head nearly brushing the ceiling. "Hardly seems fair, the number of times you've hassled me over one little incident."

"One little incident, Einar?" Leery hooked his thumb at the troll. "This genius went after a bus full of seventy-eight mundanes during his last rut and flung it right off the bridge. What was it you said, Einar? Oh, right, don't tell me. The bus *challenged* you, right?"

Einar blushed and averted his gaze. "I was mid-rut, unh. Not the best time to challenge a troll."

"Hey, a bus horn isn't exactly the same thing as a war horn, Einar."

"Not my fault. Nunnh. It sounded like one."

"You're just lucky you missed the river with it. If it had flipped into the East River, you'd have been in real trouble."

"Unh." Einar heaved a sigh, and Leery closed his eyes to the gust of wind. "What do you want, Oriscoe?"

"You know any unseelies, Einar?"

The troll curled his lip. "Distasteful bunch."

"Then you know a few of them?"

"Unh. A bugge here, a lubber there," Einar said with a shrug. "Don't like any of them." He clenched his fists, and his knuckles crackled like a string of firecrackers. "No good for eating, either, nunnnh."

"Uh, yeah. We'll take your word for it, big guy." Leery took a long sip out of his enormous cup. "So, Einar...about these unseelies. Why would one of the Brethren work with one?"

"Nunh. We wouldn't. No reason to." Einar turned his massive head to Dru and cocked it to the side. "You, though. Unnnh. I'd work with you."

"Settle down there, big man," said Leery. "You don't want to mess with her. She'd eat you for dinner."

Dru scoffed and rolled her eyes.

Einar squinted at Leery. "She's your woman? Your...bitch?"

"Now, that's not very nice language, Einar. My delicate ears are burning." Leery tossed a wink at Dru. "I think he likes you."

Einar took a threatening step toward Leery, his shoulders hunched, his massive fists floating halfway to fighting position. "I challenge you. Unh. For the woman."

Leery grimaced and took another long draught of coffee. "Relax, Einar. She's not my woman. It would do you no good to challenge me, and besides, we both know how that ended last time."

Einar growled deep in his throat. "I was mid-rut."

"Sure, sure. I bet it would be different now." Leery rolled his eyes at Dru. "Look, Einar, we just need to know a few things and then—"

"You think you would win? You think you can defeat me when I have my wits? Nunnh, I would be your doom, little human."

"Probably so, Einar, but you're forgetting my other half. The part that's neither little nor human." Leery waved his hand as though clearing the air. "Besides, I have no interest in testing the matter. You win, okay?"

"Unnnh." Einar looked at Dru askance, a smirk decorating his broad face. "I would win her."

"Einar, you're not listening. She's not mine. Okay?"

Dru glared at the troll and rattled something in the *Verba Patiendi*.

Einar took a step back, eyes widening.

"And I belong to no man."

"Unnh, Your Grace," murmured Einar. He threw an unsure glance at Leery, then dropped to one knee.

"Oh, stop that!" snapped Dru. "Just answer our questions."

"Unh. I will do as you ask, Princess Drusilla bat Argat."

"And don't call me that. Call me Detective Nogan."

Again, Einar's gaze darted to Leery's as if seeking clarification, so Leery nodded. "Do what she says, Einar."

"Unh." He rose to his feet, darting glances at Dru all the while.

"Now, tell us why one of your kind would deal with the Unseelie Court," she said.

Einar shrugged his massive shoulders, creating the illusion of two cannonballs rolling around in his shirt. "I know of no reason. Nunnh."

"Rent can't be cheap in the shadow of the bridge. Would you do it if the price were right?" Leery drained the rest of his coffee and sighed as he tossed the empty cup into the trash.

"Want more?" asked Einar.

"Sure, now that you're offering."

Einar nodded as he turned and pushed through the doors into the front of the shop.

Half a second later, the bell on the front door rang.

"Great. Customers," said Leery. "It'll take him forever."

"Mmm."

Leery leaned against the prep table, cocking his hip and grinning at Dru. "So... You're willing to expose your secret to get out of a date? Interesting."

Dru scoffed and shook her head. "He didn't have a *date* in mind, and you know it." She glanced at the double doors to the front. "Use that great hearing of yours... What do you hear?"

Leery turned his head a little, then lifted his eyebrows. "Nothing."

"Right. *Nothing.*"

"Oh, hell," Leery murmured, loosening his tie. "I left my hat back in the car."

"Maybe you can do without it?"

He pulled the horrible silk tie from his neck and tossed it at her, then went to work on the buttons of his shirt. "Sure, *I* can do without it. But my other half is devout. The question is whether *he* will do without it." The flesh of his shoulders and chest began to ripple and coarse brown-gray fur began to blossom around his neck like spring weeds.

"He'll understand."

"Yeah? You sure about that?" Leery tossed his shirt to her and kicked off his shoes.

"Can't you do this faster? Without the striptease?"

"Yeah, of course, but clothes are expensive on a cop's salary." His voice had dropped a register, and it sounded as though he had a mouthful of gravel.

"Well, you need a better system. I'm not your manservant or your maid."

Leery nodded his lupine head and stepped out of his trousers. The hair atop his head knitted itself into a perfect yarmulke, the gray hairs forming decorative patterns amongst the brown. His gaze came to rest on Dru's, and his lip curled.

"Relax, big guy. You know me."

He gave the werewolf equivalent of a scoff then held out his hand, snapping his fingers.

"Don't you two talk to each other? You forgot your hat in the car."

He growled and narrowed his eyes.

"For Abaddon's sake!" Dru gathered his pants and turned toward the door. "Go after Einar! I'll get your damn hat and catch up."

3

Leery took the back way out into the hall behind the Starbucks. He followed it to the alley without crossing paths with anyone, then lifted his snout to the sky and sniffed.

Einar's scent trail was about as obvious as a Greyhound bus in a demolition derby—three feet wide and strong enough to make his eyes water. The troll had run toward the river on the sidewalk, but Leery wanted to keep in the shadows of the alley for as long as possible. He turned away from the sidewalk and sprinted toward the intersection of the alley he was in and one that paralleled the street.

He felt the tingle of a ward settling on him like a *tallit* and snorted. *Come on. She might be Lillith-spawn, but she knows her business*, Leery thought at his wolf-brain. *If you'd give her a chance, you'd like her. The stick up her ass is almost as big as the one you carry.* Amusement colored the thoughts of his wolf-side, mixed with the primitive instinct to chase whatever had the temerity to run from him.

4

Dru sprinted out the door of the Starbucks, ignoring the stares of the people on the street. The door banged behind her. "Free coffee inside, but you'll have to help yourselves," she called as she turned toward the corner, carrying Leery's clothing balled up in front of her.

She turned onto 60th in time to see Einar's retreating back a few blocks on and sprinted diagonally to the flow of traffic. She tucked the clothes under her arm and sketched a rune set of protection in the air as she muttered the activating word of power. She glanced at the people turning to watch the troll run and the others staring at her.

She sketched another rune set in the air, and murmured an invocation of illusion, then flung it into the air, relying on its intrinsic magic to guide it to Leery.

Leaning into the turn, she rounded the corner into the alley where they'd parked and skidded to a halt behind the car. She popped the trunk open and tossed Leery's clothes inside, then grabbed his silly black hat and ran.

5

Leery trotted to the end of the alley on York Avenue and slowed to a stop. Keeping to the shadows, he peered around the corner, looking both directions. The late morning sun baked the street, providing nary a shadow, and people were everywhere, enjoying the warmth.

Can't pursue him out there. Wouldn't be prudent in this day of cell phone cameras and instant internet access. A growl rumbled in his throat. *I know, I know. The troll's getting away and all that, but what's our real choice?*

Another spell embraced him, making his hackles rise and his skin tingle. His head tilted down, and his gaze scanned up his body from his shoes to his belt. *Illusion... See? I told you she was good.*

With a puppy-like yip, he burst out of the alley and sprinted toward 60th, the scent trail there blazing like a neon god shining in the darkness. He ignored Twenty-Four Sycamores Park and trucked into the shadow of the bridge.

At the 60th Street intersection, he crossed diagonally and leaped over the chain-link fence without touching it. He landed on the roof of a trailer and stopped to sniff the air again. Einar had also climbed the fence and had then sprinted toward the building squatting in the shadow of the bridge at the riverbank. Leery threw back his head and howled.

"I'm right here, big guy," panted Dru from the sidewalk. "Here." She frisbeed his black hat up to him.

He caught it with a grunt and spun it atop his head. He pointed at the building.

"Yeah, fine. You go ahead, and I'll find a way in."

Leery glanced at the fence, then at her fashionable shoes and barked a laugh. He leaped to the sidewalk next to her, swept her up, and leaped the fence again, this time eschewing the trailer and landing amidst Einar's scent trail.

"Uh, thanks," said Dru. "Next time warn a girl."

He set her on her feet and spun away, charging through the decrepit double doors, parting the chain that held them as if its links were made from curls of paper and shattering the old wood into splinters. Einar's trail led him to a stairwell that curled downward into the darkness.

Taking the steps four at a time, Leery followed him down into the service tunnels. He sprinted, reaching his top speed in a few long strides, and raced to catch the troll, no more discomforted by the darkness as he was by moonlight.

Einar leaned against the wall in a large square room three hundred feet from the stairs, panting like a dog. Running silently as only a werewolf could, Leery came out of the darkness at him, catching him by surprise. Even so, the troll uttered a word in old Norse and swelled up like a Thanksgiving Day parade float. He reached toward Leery with both grizzly bear-sized hands, grabbing him by the shoulders.

Leery snarled and twisted his shoulders, wrenching himself inside Einar's grip, then pounced, sinking his claws into the troll's sides and burying his fangs in his trapezius.

Howling in pain and fury, Einar beat his fists against Leery's back. When that had no effect, he grabbed the werewolf by the top of the snout and wrenched his fangs away.

Growling and snapping at the troll's hands, Leery shook himself free and leaped into the darkness, planning another sneak attack.

"Unnh. You fight gud, Ulf." Einar rubbed his bleeding trapezius and laughed. "Come out and play. Unnnh. I haven't had a decent fight in a while."

Leery circled in the darkness, watching the troll flex his muscles and peer into the darkness—in the wrong direction. He sprang at Einar's back, talons and fangs extended.

6

Dru trotted down the dark tunnel using her phone's flashlight to see a feeble three feet. Ahead, snarls and grunts assaulted the stygian gloom. "Leery? You got him?"

She paused, waiting for a break in the battle sounds that didn't come. She sketched the majority of a rune set in the air, adding its neon-like glow to the light cast by her phone, and started forward.

The growling in the darkness ahead intensified, and Einar let loose a string of curses in old Norse. Something clattered and boomed against what sounded like a bank of lockers, and Leery yelped.

"Leery!" She ran into the velvet blackness, hand poised to complete the rune set, its word of power on her lips.

7

Leery held on, despite being slammed into a bank of metal lockers. He had one arm looped around Einar's throat and the other buried in his mangy mop of hair. His legs wrapped around the troll's waist, ankles hooked in front like a belt buckle.

Einar loosed a bovine-like bellow and spun in circles, trying to get at him, lost to a berserk fury. Leery shifted his grip and held on for dear life.

8

Dru slowed as the walls fell away from her sides. She lifted her phone high in the air and stopped, watching Einar spin in wild circles, Leery clinging to his back like a bronco rider.

She laughed. She couldn't help it—they looked about as silly as she could imagine a werewolf and a troll could look.

Leery glanced at her and snarled, then jerked his head toward his black hat lying at the edge of her light. Shaking her head, she completed her runes and spoke the invocation, tossing it at Einar almost as an afterthought.

The troll's manic spinning slowed, and he staggered as if carrying an immense weight. Leery looped his other arm around Einar's throat and began to squeeze. The troll ground to a stop and stooped, resting both hands on his knees.

"You can get off him now, Leery," said Dru as she bent to retrieve the hat. "He's not going anywhere until I lift the spell."

Leery's gaze found hers, and he cocked his head to the side like any dog hearing a strange word.

"Down boy," Dru said with a smile.

With narrowed eyes, Leery leaped away. He straightened and stalked toward her, holding his hand out. When she dropped the hat in his palm, he grunted and put it on his head with a flourish.

"Now, Einar. If you ever want to move from this room again, you'll answer our questions."

Leery growled in support.

Einar's black-eyed glare darted from the werewolf's face to hers. "Nunnh. You cheat."

"Not at all, you just brought brute strength to a rune fight. Surely you can appreciate the irony?" Dru flashed her best smile at him. "Now, I believe Leery asked you whether one of the Brethren would work with an unseelie if the money were right. What's the answer?"

Einar dropped his gaze and struggled against her spell, straightening his back and taking a single step toward the hall. "Unnh. You see? I can leave if I want?"

"Whatever you need to tell yourself. Answer the question."

The troll sneered and glowered at her, then stooped his back with a gasp and again rested his hands on his knees. "Nunnh. I wouldn't work with unseelie bugs. Not me. But they came to me with their offer."

"They did? Who?" Dru glanced at Leery. "You can change back."

Leery glared at her a moment, his lip twitching, then nodded and began his change.

"Nunh. Don't know who. Unseelie bugs."

"What kind of unseelie? What did they look like?"

"Bugs. Unnh." His gaze tracked to Leery, eyes narrowing at the spectacle. "Undignified," he muttered.

"You'll have to do better than that, Einar. You assaulted my partner." Dru waved a lazy hand at Leery. "You ran. Both of those spell five years."

"Spell five years? Nunh. You're a strange one."

"Five years in the dungeon beneath Rikers."

Einar grunted and went to one knee. "Take this off."

"No. As of right now, you're under arrest, and I don't want to chase you again."

"Come on, Einar," growled Leery. He stood next to Dru, black hat held in front of his waist.

"I said I don't know the unseelie bugs. Can't describe them—too ugly. But..."

"But?" asked Dru.

"Am I under arrest? Nunnh."

Leery stepped forward. "Einar, you help us, and I'll talk her out of taking you in."

"No, Leery! He's—" Dru stamped her foot.

"Einar?" Leery quirked a bushy eyebrow at him.

"Unnh, fine. They talked to Lothidn, too. Unh. He wanted money more than me."

"Fine. Where do we find Lothidn?" asked Dru.

"In the shadow of a bridge," said Einar. He grunted and went down on both knees. "Unnh. Now, let me up!"

"That's not helpful, Einar. You should—"

"Is that the same Lothidn who does the underground fights at the butchery?"

Einar nodded, sweat beading on his brow. "Unnh."

"I know where to find him," Leery said. "You can let him go."

"Right. But no funny business, Einar, or I'll put it right back on and leave it for a day."

Einar grunted. "Unnh."

Dru lifted the rune set, then led the two back the way they'd come.

They made a strange trio, exiting the smashed double doors of the building. Einar groaned at the mess and kicked the broken chain that had held the doors closed. "You broke my doors."

"Shouldn't have locked them," said Leery in a cheerful voice.

"You pay."

"Nunh," said Leery. He walked hunched over, hat held in front of his privates.

Dru grinned at him. "The illusion is still working, Leery."

"Fine, fine, but does it work on you?"

Eyes twinkling, Dru shrugged. "That would be telling. No?"

"Very funny." He looked at Einar askance. "Gee, I wish there was a Starbucks open around here. I could sure use a cup of coffee."

"More?" groaned Einar. "Do you piss coffee?"

"Hey, don't knock it until you've tried it, Einar. Besides, it keeps my wolf strong and ready."

Einar grimaced. "I go. Unnh. Buy doors."

"Have fun," said Leery, starting across the street.

"You owe me, unnh?"

Leery shook his head. "You still *owe* me, Einar. It doesn't count if you make me chase you down and wrestle."

9

Snugging his spare tie up to the collar of his spare shirt, Leery slid behind the wheel of his Crown Vic. Dru already sat in the passenger seat, her gaze tracking his movements.

"How do we find this Lothidn?"

"There's an underground fighting ring in a meat packing plant across the river. The guy who runs it is an old CI of mine. He'll know where to find Lothidn."

"Do you literally know everyone in this Locus' seedy underbelly?"

"That's what they pay me for." Leery threw the car into reverse and gunned it out onto 60th Street—without looking. Tires screeched and horns blew, but Leery continued on as if he couldn't hear a thing.

"Maybe I should drive from now on," muttered Dru.

"Nah, we don't have time for me to teach you how to drive New York style."

Dru rolled her eyes and turned to watch the sidewalk sail past.

"Before we get on the bridge, I need a coffee."

Scoffing, Dru snapped her head back around. "I thought you were kidding."

"I never kid about coffee, Nogan. *Never*."

"Right. Swing by the Starbucks."

"But Einar's not there."

"Yeah, which means you can serve yourself as much coffee as you can drink."

"Hmm. Is it stealing if the place is left open but unattended?" Leery circled back on 61st Street. "Or is it looting?"

"We'll leave money on the counter."

"What, and let some unscrupulous person rob the place?" Leery shook his head. "No, I'll leave Einar a note. An IOU."

"Right." Dru snapped one hand to the dash and the other to the door frame as Leery turned onto 1st Avenue against the flow of the one-way traffic. "Are you nuts?" she cried.

"Oh, right." He flipped on the dash spinner and the siren. "Safety first."

10

Leery pulled up to the corner of the sidewalk at the intersection of 11th Street and 45th Road, blocking the crosswalk in both directions. He threw the car in park and popped open his door.

"You can't be serious," murmured Dru.

"Come on, Nogan. You should know by now that I can always find a space, no matter how bad the parking gets."

"This *isn't* a space, Oriscoe."

"You say tomato…" He stepped from the car and slammed the door, walking around the back and stepping up on the curb. He opened her door. "Come on, Dru. I gave you the sidewalk side, didn't I?"

She covered her eyes with her palm for a moment, shaking her head. Then she heaved a sigh and got out. Dru glanced up at the three-foot-tall wooden letters that adorned the seedy-looking building. "John Michael May Meat Packing," it read.

"Come on, Nogan. It ain't the Ritz, but it's where I can find my CI."

"He works here?"

"Nah. He owns the place. It's a front for his fighting game." Leery turned and walked up the sidewalk to the building's glass doors. He opened one side for her and stood waiting like a doorman until she walked through.

The lobby of the building looked as though it had been jerked right out of 1972. The avocado-hued vinyl-upholstered chairs had tears repaired with silver duct tape, and the multicolored shag area rug was enough to blind a man—done in bright orange, lime green, and gray. Cheap, dark-colored paneling covered the walls, adorned with horrible prints of dogs playing poker. Even the receptionist's counter was covered in cheap Formica, and the rotary phone was harvest gold.

"I didn't know rotary phones still worked."

"They don't," said Leery with a grimace. "It's window dressing."

"Not very good window dressing."

Leery lifted his shoulders and let them fall. "Follow me. May's back here." He pushed his way through a pair of white swinging doors that had almost turned red with ingrained, grimy blood.

The room beyond the reception area had been the butchery in better times. Old stainless-steel worktops ringed the room, and empty hooks hung from tracks set in the ceiling. A sharpening station rested on its side against the back wall, and a band-saw missing its blade stood in the corner like a forgotten child on punishment. Gunk and sludge hazed the harvest gold tiles underfoot. Another set of swinging doors led to the warehouse beyond. A large freezer door stood ajar to their right, and a single door lay to the left.

Leery sniffed and wrinkled his nose. "This way." He walked to the single door and pulled it open to reveal a staircase leading to the second floor. As they tromped up the stairs, the surroundings changed from 1972 chic to modern Scandinavian designs—all black, chrome, and pale wood.

A man stood in the center of the room, arms akimbo.

"May!" called Leery. "You missed me?"

The man scoffed, scowling. "Leery. Aren't you dead yet?"

"No such luck, pal. How's business? Still running your little fights?"

May's gaze darted to Dru, laden with suspicion. "Who's this, Oriscoe?"

"Relax, John. This is my new partner, Dru Nogan. Dru, meet John. He's a fight promoter."

Leery made quote fingers as he said the last bit.

"I'll have you know I fill a need that no one else does, Leery. It's simple economics."

"Sure thing, professor. Listen up, May. We need to talk to one of your fighters."

May tilted his head to the side, eyes narrowing. "Why?"

"Let us worry about why, John," said Dru in a soft, sexy voice.

He spared her a single glance that lasted all of three seconds. "Succubus?" he asked Leery.

Dru's face wrinkled in confusion.

"Nah. We want to talk to one of your trolls. Fellow named Lothidn."

May rolled his eyes. "I meant your partner, Oriscoe."

"Yeah, I figured that out, May." He arched both eyebrows. "Lothidn?"

May threw another short glance at Dru and wrinkled his nose. "It's my nature to pierce illusions."

"And what nature is that?"

"May used to be *Shuten-doji*, Dru."

She cast a blank gaze in Leery's direction.

"I'm the offspring of an *Oni*."

"A Japanese ogre?"

May shrugged. "More of a demon, but you may call them what you will."

"Okay."

"Remember when you told me who is immune to your charms?"

Dru nodded, studying May's face.

"Incubi, immune humans, and vampires, you said."

"Yes."

"*Shuten-doji* survives off the blood of the injured."

"Ah!" Dru's face transformed with a sunny smile. "That explains it."

May turned to Leery. "Lesson's over. Why do you want Lothidn?"

"His name came up in an investigation."

May lifted a single eyebrow, his gaze intensifying.

"Your tricks won't work on me, May. You know that."

He smiled and gave a little shrug, as if to say you can't blame me for trying. "I guess it doesn't matter in any case. Lothidn has left the fight game."

"Oh?" asked Leery.

"Yes. He got a better offer he said. Something where the blood wasn't his." May turned and stared out the window. "He wanted a better quality of life, it seems."

"You have his address?"

May gestured toward the bridge. "He lives in the Queens Bridge Housing complex. Off 41st and 10th Street. Second floor. Right by the staircase."

"It's not bad anymore. Green space, events, gardening."

"He wanted a bigger place, I guess. He is a troll, after all."

"Right."

"But don't bother heading over there."

Leery arched an eyebrow.

"He already moved. I have no idea to where."

"You could have led with that, May."

John smiled and winked.

I I

Leery pulled the cruiser's two passenger wheels up on the sidewalk outside the precinct house and killed the ignition. He glanced at Dru, eyebrow quirked.

"No," she said. "I've given up."

"You learn quick, kid."

"I sure do, Old Spice."

"Right, I forgot." He grinned and opened his door. "Come on. Time to inaugurate you into one of the SIS traditions: Lunch with the lieu."

"But I don't eat."

"Yeah, I know that, Nogan, but I *do*. It's more of a working lunch, anyway." They made their way to the squad room, Leery holding a fresh cup of coffee and a sandwich from the vending machines in the lobby. He bypassed their desks in favor of Lieutenant Van Helsing's office and slumped into one of her guest chairs.

Dru paused at the door, scanning the office, which appeared empty. She sank into the other chair, her gaze slinking around the room, looking for any disturbance in the air that might give away the lieu's presence.

"Relax, Nogan," said Van Helsing's disembodied voice. She appeared in the corner behind her desk, up near the ceiling, and floated down to sit in her chair. She spared Leery and his sandwich a glance, then turned her gaze to Dru. "Not eating? Don't fast on my behalf."

Dru fidgeted, her gaze dropping to her lap.

"Oh, that's right," crooned the lieutenant. "Your meals involve coitus."

Dru sniffed but held her tongue.

"Come on, Lieu," said Leery through a mouthful of egg salad.

"I can't believe you eat egg salad out of those disgusting machines, Oriscoe."

"Hey, I like egg salad. And it's not as though it'll kill me if it's bad." He took a gulp of coffee and smacked his lips. "Plus, this vending machine coffee is guaranteed to kill anything that can be killed—bacteria included."

Van Helsing shook her head, then turned her gaze back to Dru, her lip starting to curl.

"Anyway. We made some progress on the Willams-Costello murders." He downed another mouthful of egg salad and coffee. "Then we hit a wall."

"Oh?" Van Helsing arched an eyebrow, her gaze boring into Dru's.

"We have a name: Lothidn. He's another Norwegian Wood Troll, and we're told he was amenable to working with the unseelie." Dru returned Van Helsing's gaze with a calm, graceful demeanor.

"Oh?" the lieu repeated.

"Sure," said Leery. "It seems he wanted a better apartment, so he was open to opportunities involving larger sums than he could make in illegal fights."

Epatha's head snapped around. "*Shuten-doji* is involved?"

Leery shook his head. "It doesn't look like it. Lothidn worked for him but left for the new opportunity."

The lieu's eyes narrowed. "Still. I don't like it. *Shuten-doji* organized that massacre back in Japan. He bears watching."

"He left all that behind, Lieu," said Leery.

"So *he* says."

"Right. I've got my eye on him, just in case. Besides, he was helpful this time."

"Helpful and truthful aren't the same thing. You can't trust the word of a demon's offspring." She turned her head at a languid pace to stare at Dru.

"Come on, Lieu," said Leery, dribbling egg salad into his lap. "She's done good. You know she has. Cut her a break."

Epatha sighed and pursed her lips. "Yeah," she sighed. "I'm having a bad day."

"Anything we can do?" asked Leery.

"Not a thing. But thanks." Van Helsing closed her translucent eyelids for a moment, her gaze remaining locked on Leery's. "What's the wall you hit?"

"May knew his old address but said Lothidn had already moved on. He doesn't know where to."

"That's not a wall, Leery. You know he has to live in the shadow of a bridge."

"Sure, Lieu, but which bridge? Anyway, there's got to be thousands of apartments in the shadow of one of the city's bridges."

"Have you heard of computers, Oriscoe? They're these almost magic doodads that let you find information quickly. The department even has some."

Leery wagged his head back and forth. "Yeah, yeah. We're getting to that right after lunch."

Epatha arched an eyebrow. "It seems like you're the only one eating, Leery."

"Hey, I can't help it you're dead, and she eats... Well, I can't help it if I'm the only one that needs food. I need it, regardless."

"And we're here to keep you company?" Van Helsing tipped a wink at Dru.

"Sure. It's a working lunch."

"Mmm-hmm. Get to work, Leery."

12

Leery thumped his laptop. "I can't make this damn thing work." He snarled at the screen and slid his fingers across the keyboard in random directions. "There, you bastard. Try that for my password."

Hiding a smile, Dru slid her chair around to his side of their paired desks. "Here. Let me try."

"Be my guest," said Leery, pushing away from the laptop. "But the damn thing's broken, I'm telling you."

Dru clacked a few keys and clicked the mouse. "There you go, Leery," she said, ducking her head so he couldn't see her amusement.

"How in the..." He peered down at the screen. "How'd you do that? Even I don't know my password."

"I took a guess."

"A guess? Fess up. You used your magic, right?"

"No. You've never changed your password from the default algorithm."

"Algorithm? Default? Why didn't someone tell me?" He glared around the room.

"I wrote it on your pad there. You should change it to something you'll remember."

"Right, like I know how to do that."

Dru smiled at him. "I'll show you when we get back."

"From where?"

"I've got Lothidn's address from the Locus Census Bureau. We should take backup so we don't have to chase him, too."

13

Leery and Dru stood against the wall in the corridor outside Lothidn's apartment, standing behind the Servitor Warriors and Therianthropes entry team. Composed of two translucent humans in glowing body armor—servitor warriors for a pair of wizards outside in the command vehicle—and four therianthropes: a Ketuan skin-walker, a young werewolf, a Garudan, and leading them all, a Ganeshan.

The Ganeshan turned his elephantine head to look at Leery, flapping his giant ears in agitation. Thick muscles and limbs filled out his wide human body, giving him the look of something out of a comic book.

"What?" Leery whispered.

With a glance at the eagle-headed Garudan, the Ganeshan snorted through his trunk.

"Which door?" grated one of the servitors.

"29B," said Dru.

The Ganeshan nodded and turned toward the door.

"You have a team covering the back?" asked Leery.

"Yes," said the servitor in a strange voice that brought ringing bells to mind. "Stay back. We'll tell you when it's clear."

"Claw and Warder, remember?" said Dru. "We'll come in with you."

The Ketuan skin-walker crossed both sets of arms and shook his head, swaying slightly on the snake's tail that served as his lower body. "We've got this. You'd get in the way," he said.

"But—"

The young werewolf glared at Dru through narrowed eyelids and growled.

"Fine," said Leery, laying his hand on Dru's arm. "We'll wait here."

With a grunt, the Ganeshan lowered his head and charged the door, slamming into it with his tusks and massive forehead. He jerked his head up and back, ripping the door out of its frame, while spinning out of the way with the grace of a dancer. The servitor warriors slid through the wall in absolute silence.

With an ear-piercing screech, the Garudan charged through the door with the young wolf hot on his heels. The Ketuan slithered in behind them, a shotgun in his upper pair of hands and two pistols in the lower set.

Dru stepped toward the door, peering inside. "Come on, Leery. Let's get in there."

"No, Dru, wait for the all-clear signal. No reason for us to get sweaty. SWAT is on it."

The Ganeshan shook the remains of the door from his tusks and glared at them, holding up a hand and shaking his head.

A basso bellow sounded from the depths of the apartment, followed by a crash and the shriek of the Garudan. The Ganeshan lowered his head and tusks, then pelted into the apartment.

Dru almost danced in place, her gaze locked on the open door. "I hate standing out here while they have all the fun."

"Hey, they have all the risk, too. It's what they live for, Dru. Let them do their jobs."

Dru grunted and took a step forward. "I never pegged you for a coward, Leery."

"Coward? Nah. I'll take what risks I have to, but there's no reason to take unnecessary ones." He blew out a breath. "Relax, Dru. It'll only take them a minute."

A crash of thunder came from the doorway followed by a heavy grunt and another cacophony of broken furniture and glass. Then, silence.

One of the servitors stuck his head through the wall. "Come on in," he said in metallic tones.

"Finally," Dru muttered and strode through the door. With a wry grin, Leery followed her.

The apartment was a wreck. Broken furniture littered the main room, and a massive hole in the drywall added a new door to the master suite. The four therianthropes lay in a pile at the foot of the overlarge bed.

Dru and Leery entered through the hole in the wall, stepping over shards of glass from a broken mirror and the coffee table's top. "Is Lothidn under there?" asked Leery with a grin.

"Cuffs!" snapped the Ketuan, holding out a hand from the dogpile.

"Better use two sets," said Leery. He held out his hand for Dru's set, while drawing his own set out of the leather case he wore in the small of his back.

Dru slapped her cuffs in his hand and turned toward the bathroom suite. "Is the place clear?"

"Yes," said one of the servitors. "We cleared the rest of the apartment while the therianthropes apprehended the suspect."

"Well, good," said Dru in a quiet voice.

Leery put the handcuffs into the skin-walker's hand. "Relax down there, Lothidn. We have a few questions for you and decided you'd be more comfortable down at the station."

A moment of silence followed, punctuated by the clicking of two pairs of handcuffs. "Unnh. What do you want?"

The werewolf rolled off the pile, followed by the Garudan, who took a moment to smooth his feathers.

"We'll get to that when we're all comfortable and drinking coffee. You do like coffee, right, Lothidn?"

"Unh, sure."

"Good. Relax, and we'll get this straightened out."

"I don't like handcuffs. Nunnh."

Dru puffed a sigh between her pursed lips. "Why did we come along? I hate feeling useless."

"Relax, Dru. I'll get you a cup, too."

14

Leery pushed through the interview room door with his shoulder, carrying a tray filled with four cups of coffee. Dru sat across the small table from Lothidn, who, if anything, was even bigger than Einar. He dwarfed her and the table, both, and made the room feel like a closet.

"Well, isn't this cozy?" asked Leery as he set the drink tray in the middle of the table. He grabbed one of the extra-large steaming Styrofoam cups and took a sip. "Mmm. Just like Mom used to make." He nodded at Dru's cell phone lying on the table. "Get his picture?"

Dru clicked her tongue and crossed her arms. "Of course."

"This is the one with seventy-eight sugars," he said, tapping the cup closest to her.

"I'll pass, thanks."

"Lothidn?"

"Unnh." The troll leaned forward and took one of the cups, which looked very small in his large mitt.

"Now, Lothidn, we understand you recently left John Michael May's employ?"

"Unh. But that's not his name."

"Yeah, we know. *Shuten-doji*. But you gave up the fight game?"

"No competition. Nunh." He rolled his massive shoulders.

"Come on, Lothidn. The way we heard it— from two separate sources, mind you—you, uh, got a better offer."

Lothidn drew his mouth into a severe line. "Who told you that?"

"It doesn't matter. The point is: we *know*."

Again, the Norwegian Wood Troll shrugged his shoulders. "Then why you ask me?"

"It establishes trust and rapport when you answer with the truth. When you lie, we know you're a liar, so…"

The troll chuckled—a sound like boulders grating together in a bad storm.

"What was the offer?" asked Dru, leaning forward and tapping the table.

"Nunh. I think I want a magister."

"What do you need a magister for? All I asked is about your new job."

Lothidn scratched his stubble-covered chin. "Unnh, but maybe I don't want to tell you."

"Why not, Lothidn?" asked Dru, her voice laced with a sweetness usually reserved for virgins.

The troll glanced at her, then averted his eyes. "Nunh."

"What's the matter? You've never seen a beautiful woman before?" asked Leery with a grin for Dru.

"Unnnh. I've seen beautiful females. Rutted with them." He grunted and waved a hand at Dru. "She's too small. Too...delicate. Nunnh. I'd hurt her."

"Oh, you'd be surprised, Lothidn. In fact, I'd say you were the one in danger of injury." Leery rubbed his shoulder. "Take it from me. Her kind can get rough in the bedroom."

"Unnnnh," sighed Lothidn. He turned his gaze back on Dru and examined every inch of her he could see.

A small smile played on Dru's lips, and she touched the tip of her tongue to the center of her upper lip. A buzzing noise issued from her open mouth, and Lothidn tensed, eyes open very wide.

"Hey, Dru, I think he likes you."

"I *know* he likes me, Leery," she said in a sultry voice, her gaze locked on Lothidn's. "But I'm not sure I like him."

"Oh, don't go hurting his feelings."

If Lothidn heard their exchange, he gave no sign. His nutmeg-colored skin flushed and sweat beaded on his brow.

Dru's eyes sparkled, and she pushed herself away from the table. "No," she said in a suddenly cold voice. "I don't like men who keep secrets."

Lothidn reacted as if she'd slapped him, pulling his chin back and frowning. "Nunh. You play a dangerous game."

Van Helsing floated through the mirrored window and crooked her finger at Dru. "Outside, now."

Leery blew out his breath and stood. He and Dru crossed to the door to the observation room and went through it.

"Lieu, we were getting somewhere—"

"Shut it, Leery!" snapped Van Helsing. She flickered invisible, and when she reappeared a heartbeat later, she stood three inches from Dru, a ghostly finger held straight up. "What did you think you were doing in there, strumpet?"

"Interviewing the suspect."

"Oh, is that what that little display was?" The corner of the lieu's mouth turned down. "That's funny, because to me it appeared you were *seducing* that troll."

Dru shook her head.

"Don't deny it!"

"Come on, Lieu," said Leery. "The Canon and Covenants allow us to use our natural gifts in all phases of an invest—"

Flickering in and out of view, Van Helsing held up her palm. "Don't you dare, Oriscoe. Don't you dare quote the C and C to me. The tart's behavior goes beyond the pale." She turned away from them both and began to pace, still fluttering in and out of phase with the visible spectrum. "Dangerous! Irresponsible!"

"No, I was in complete control of the situation."

"Don't give me that, harlot."

"Name-calling is beneath your dignity, Lieu," said Leery.

"Is it?" Van Helsing disappeared and reappeared facing him half a heartbeat later, snapped her fingers in his face, then disappeared and reappeared close to Dru again. "That troll is close to rut. Didn't you see the signs?"

"Of course, I did," said Dru with a little heat in her voice. "That's why I turned up the wattage."

"And if he'd lost control? If he'd suddenly fallen into rut because of your '*wattage*?'"

Dru shrugged. "He's not *that* close."

"Oh, no? And you are certain of this, how?"

A one-sided smile—more of a sneer—appeared on Dru's lips. "Because of who and what I am, Van Helsing. I'm the one best suited for evaluating such matters."

"Dangerous!"

"Everything was under *my* control."

"*Reckless!*"

"Not at all. I know precisely where the line is, Lieutenant. I wasn't even close."

"In this precinct, *I* define where that line is, not some avaricious, bawdy little libertine!"

Dru opened her mouth to retort, her face twisted with anger, her eyes narrowed.

Van Helsing held up a hand. "No more, siren. No more! Watch how this can be done without resorting to base tactics!" She flickered away and reappeared in the interview room. She glanced at the mirrored window. "Leery, get your posterior in here."

Leery sighed and took a giant gulp of coffee. "For what it's worth, Dru, I think you played it right."

"Yeah," she hissed. "Not that what you or I think matters."

"Well... The lieu's got this whole Victorian thing going. She can't help it. Those were the times she was raised in."

"By prudes!"

"Worse. *Paladins.*"

"Leery!" Van Helsing shouted.

"Oops, gotta go." He returned to the interview room, taking another swig of coffee, and closed the door behind him.

"Where is the other one?" asked Lothidn.

"She won't be returning," said Van Helsing in a gelid tone.

"Nunnh. Then get my magister." The troll crossed his arms over his ample chest muscles and leaned back in his chair.

"Oh, now you've done it, Lothidn," said Leery, shaking his head sadly. "Now, we can't help you get out of the mess you're in."

"Nunh. No mess. Magister."

"Come on, Lothidn. Let's not blow all this out of proportion."

"M-A-G-I-S-T-E-R."

Van Helsing glared at the troll, flashing and fading in turns. "Bad move, troll," she hissed.

"You really should try to cooperate," said Leery.

"Nunnh. Magister. Now."

Van Helsing growled and disappeared.

"Great," muttered Leery. "How about I go see if Dru can come back?"

"Too late," said Lothidn, shaking his big head. "Get me a magister or I'm leaving. Or do you charge me with a crime?"

Leery sighed. "No, no charges at this time."

"Fine. I'm leaving. Unnh. Don't follow me. Don't come wreck my apartment again. Nunnh." Lothidn pushed back from the table, and Leery had to dive for the tray of coffees to keep them from spilling.

"Whew, that was close," he said as Lothidn swept out the door.

15

Dru slammed the door shared by the observation room and the squad room and stalked to her desk. She slumped into her chair and glared at Van Helsing's office door. Her face settled into a cold mask, and she fished her cell phone from the pocket of her coat before stalking out of the room.

Leery came out of the interview room in time to see her breezing toward the elevator. "Hey, Dru. You want your coffee?"

"You have it, Oriscoe," she said over her shoulder.

"Where are you going?"

The elevator doors slid shut.

Leery sniffed and threw a glance at Van Helsing's office. He set the tray of coffee on his desk, stepped toward the lieutenant's office, then turned back and took a second cup of joe in his free hand. "Gonna need this, I think," he muttered.

He stepped through Van Helsing's door, his gaze floating around the room. "I know you're in here, Lieu," he said softly. "Come on out. We need to talk."

"Why? So you can tell me how wrong I am?" said Epatha's disembodied voice. "I've been hearing nothing else lately—and from more important men than you."

"What's all this about, Epatha?" Leery sank into his accustomed chair and took a sip each from his two cups of coffee. "You've been on edge."

"Ha! You think so?" Van Helsing materialized in her chair, her head cradled in her hands. "First, I'm forced—*forced*, Leery— into accepting that...that cocotte into my squad, then I'm chastised for dealing with her failures as I see fit. Tell me that's not a fine kettle of mackerel."

"By who?"

"By the Chief of Ds, by the Commissioner, even by his eminence, the Cynosure. It seems she has powerful friends."

Leery squinted at the lieutenant over one of his coffee cups. "More than that, Lieu. But I don't think Dru called in any reinforcements. It's not in her character."

"Oh, isn't it?"

"No, Epatha, it isn't." Leery shook his head and took a gulp of coffee. "Look, Lieu, she's using an officially sanctioned fake name to avoid favoritism. Her family—"

"*This* is her avoiding favoritism?" demanded Van Helsing, shaking a sheath of paper at Leery.

"I don't know what that is, Lieu, but I've seen her anger when her identity is threatened."

"Yeah, I heard all about her performance in Crowley's courtroom."

"Hey, it's not like she could control the judge. She had to go along with his antics, but she didn't like it. Besides, Old Crowley is like an uncle to her."

"Who is she, Leery?"

"I can't tell you that, Lieu, but maybe you should just ask her."

Van Helsing flickered like a bulb about to go out and sighed. "Sure. Maybe I should bend the knee, as well."

"I can't tell you more, Lieu, so please don't ask, but you're not far from the truth there."

She looked at him for a long moment, then nodded to herself. "Half-succubus, half-vampire."

Leery drank his coffee and said nothing.

"Oh, no," said Van Helsing in a miserable tone. "Tell me she's not who I think she is."

"Like I said, Lieu. I can't say anything."

The lieutenant seemed to shrink in on herself until she disappeared from view. Leery shrugged and left her office.

16

Leery hung up the phone and grinned at Dru as she walked into the squad room. "Feeling better?"

Dru looked at the lieutenant's office with a sour, angry expression on her face. "Sure. Peachy."

"Listen, Dru. She's getting pressure from on high."

"And?"

"Pressure about you, and it rankles."

"I haven't asked anyone to—"

"Doesn't matter. She's getting flak from the Chief of Ds, the Police Commissioner, even the Cynosure."

"*What*?" Dru grimaced at the ground and brought her hands up to rub her temples.

"That's right."

"Then she's right? I don't belong here, do I, Leery?"

"No, that part's wrong. You've got great instincts for this work, Dru. But people are out to help you regardless of your subterfuge about the names."

"*Mother*," Dru groaned.

"That'd be my guess, though His Majesty the Prince might bear his share of blame there. I know if you were my daughter, I'd be pulling favors from here to Sunday to get you what you wanted."

Dru slumped into her chair. "Who was that? On the phone."

"Hinton. I called her in to see if one of the victims can ID Lothidn from the picture you took of him."

"Good thinking."

"Listen, Dru. You should speak to Van Helsing. Lay it all out on the table. Let her know you don't want any of this interference that's been plaguing her. Tell her you'll speak to your parents." Leery waved his hand in a vague circle. "You know, all that."

"Right." Her face hardened. "I hate this, Leery."

"I know you do."

"Get me when Hinton shows up, okay? I want to be in on the séance."

"Righto. Oh, look. There's that coffee I brought you."

"Knock yourself out, Leery."

Dru walked to the lieutenant's door and knocked. "Lieutenant Van Helsing? You got a second?"

"Come in and close the door."

Leery smiled as the door swung shut. "I should hang out a shingle. Maybe do couples counseling." He sobered after a moment. "Then again, my third wife would probably say I'm not cut out for it." He shrugged and reached for Dru's coffee.

17

Jenn Hinton swept into the squad room like a whirlwind, a large black case in one hand, and her many-colored long scarf in the other. Her delicate features wore a smile that was almost fetching, but all that faded as she dropped the scarf onto Dru's desk and the illusion it bore faded, revealing her true features—hunched back, maroon scales, enormous feet. "Ready to do this thing, Oriscoe?"

"One second." He picked up his phone and punched in Van Helsing's extension. "Yeah, Lieu? My nemesis is here for the séance. What? Yeah, Hinton, from CSI. Right." He hung up the phone and flashed a grin at Jenn. "Let's get you set up."

Jenn's eyes went to the closed door, and she raised an eyebrow.

"Nothing to worry about," said Leery.

Hinton shrugged. "Interview room?"

"Yeah, it ain't the Ritz, but it's the best we've got." He led her to the door and held it open for her.

She looked at him with narrow-eyed suspicion. "What's up?"

"I don't know what you mean."

"The last time you were nice to me, you wanted me to summon Elvis. I'll tell you the same thing I told you then: He's too busy."

"Forget about that, would you? It was an errant thought."

"Then why are you being so nice?"

"Fine," he said. He walked into the room and closed the door in her face.

With a small grin, she followed him inside. "That's better."

"Yep." He leaned against the window ledge and waved at the table. "Hurry up, will you?"

"These things take time, Oriscoe." She plodded to the table and stood looking down at it for a few breaths before lifting her case and setting it on the table. Then she looked at that for a moment before working the clasps.

"I think you've gotten even slower than you used to be."

"Why thank you, Leery," said Jenn.

Van Helsing and Dru came in from the observation room, both smiling.

Hinton pulled a pendulum from her case and set it in the center of the table. "We'll need the photo."

84   ERIK HENRY VICK

"I've got it on my phone."

"No physical copy?"

Dru shook her head.

Hinton sighed. "We'll make do. Keep it ready, and when I say, show it to the spirit."

Van Helsing scoffed at the pendulum. "You don't need that thing."

"It helps me focus," said Hinton with a shrug. She brought out her chalk and bent to sketch a pentagram under the table. When she straightened up, she pulled a black candle from her bag and lit it before setting it down next to the pendulum. "Ready?"

Leery and Dru took seats on one side of the table, and Hinton sat in a chair opposite them. "Lieutenant? Do you wish to participate? It might be uncomfortable."

"I'll observe from in there." She hooked her thumb toward the mirrored window and disappeared.

"Right. Who wants to hold the pendulum?"

"Uh, it's for you, right?"

Hinton leaned forward and held a hand cupped to her mouth. She whispered, "Not really, but I make it practice not to argue with ghosts about how to summon them. They all have their own ideas on the subject, and frankly, they should leave it to professionals."

"Ah," said Leery. He picked up the pendulum and held it out to Dru, who shook her head. "I guess it's me, then."

"Fine. As much as I dislike the idea, we need to join hands." She took Leery by the wrist holding the pendulum. "It's important that we don't break contact."

"Why all the hocus pocus? Why can't you summon them as you did in the alley?" asked Dru.

"They've gone on," said Jenn with a shrug. "I can't just call them back. I'll need to send a spirit for them." She held out her hand.

With a sigh, Dru took it, then grabbed Leery's empty hand.

"Aw, shucks. Does this mean we're going steady?" Leery grinned at both women.

"Is he always this immature?" asked Dru.

"Only around women. And most men. And animals."

Leery cocked his head to the side, smiled, and batted his eyelashes. "Let's go, Hinton. I don't have all day."

"Fine. Here we go." Hinton closed her eyes and hummed a single note. "Are there any helper spirits nearby? Is there anyone willing to speak with us today? If so, please swing the pendulum." Everyone stared at the prism hanging from its thin silver chain. "Please assist us," Jenn intoned. "We need your help. If you are willing, please touch the prism."

After a moment, the pendulum swung back and forth.

"Thank you," said Jenn. "We need to speak with two spirits who recently transitioned to the spirit world. In our realm, they were known as Michelle Williams and Katy Costello. Can you locate them for us? If you can, please swing the pendulum toward me." She waited until it moved toward her, then nodded. "Thank you. Please ask either one to come to this spot and manifest."

After a few minutes, the air above the candle began to shimmer and pulse with soft blue light. The swirling mist coalesced into the head of Katy Costello. Her lips moved, but she made no sound.

"One moment," said Hinton. She leaned back and closed her eyes. After a breath, she chanted something in the *Verba Patiendi*. Opening her eyes, she nodded at Costello. "There. You should have enough form to move the required air molecules."

"Can you hear me now?"

"Yes. Ms. Costello. We have a photograph we'd like to show you. Detective Nogan has it on her phone."

Katy nodded. "Fine."

Dru held up the phone, and Katy stared at for a few seconds. "It's hard to see, but that's him."

"Are you sure?" asked Leery.

"I'll never forget him," said Katy as she began to fade in and out. "That bastard amputated my arms with a pair of battle axes."

"Right."

"Thank you, Ms. Costello," intoned Hinton.

"Will I have to return to testify?" the ghost asked.

"No, that won't be necessary. Your identification here is enough."

"Good. This is harder than I thought it would be." She grinned, but it wasn't a happy one. "Otherwise, I'd haunt that bastard troll."

18

Leery stepped into Van Helsing's open doorway. "He's in the wind, Lieu. He must've run out of here and never stopped running."

"That's not good."

"No, it isn't, but Dru has an idea."

"Oh?" The lieu appeared out of thin air, facing him through the doorway.

"Yeah. Tell her, Dru."

"Financial records, Lieu. We know he got paid for what he did, so we can check his bank accounts for—"

"No. He'd have insisted on cash. Either that or his employers would have."

Dru's face fell. "Yeah, I suppose you're right."

"What should we do, then?" asked Leery with a shrug and a sour look.

"Oh, I don't know... Try police work?"

"Right."

Van Helsing chuckled, a warm, relaxed sound like the babbling of a brook. "I do have an idea for you."

"All ears, Lieu. All ears."

Epatha's glowing face stretched with a smile. "*Shuten-doji*. He knows more than he told you. I'd bet on it."

"I don't know, Lieu. I've known him for years now, and he's been reliable as an informant."

"But I bet none of the cases he helped you on hurt him or his business. Am I right?"

Leery shoved his hands in his pants pockets. "Well, yeah, but he—"

"No, I think she's right, Leery," said Dru. "Something about that whole interview felt...*off*."

Leery's gaze swung back and forth between them like Hinton's pendulum, then he shrugged. "Then let's go grab him up."

"Bring him back here," said Van Helsing. "Put him in holding for an hour or two. I'll see if I can arrange a suitable welcome."

"Oh, boy," said Leery. "That sounds so ominous when you say it, Lieu."

"Bet your ass, Leery."

19

John May stood in the holding cell, hands tight on the bars to either side of his face. His eyes burned with anger as Leery stepped away from the door. "Why are you doing this, Oriscoe?"

"Come on, May. You know why."

"No, I don't think I do."

"Why is it I have the feeling you haven't been forthcoming with *all* that you know?"

"Because you're an idiot?"

"Oh, now you've hurt my feelings, May. Didn't your mother ever teach you this one: 'Sticks and stones may break my bones, but names will never hurt me?'"

"*Kutabare, koshinuke,*" snarled May.

"Come on, *Shuten-doji*. If you're going to insult me, use a language I understand. It's more fun that way."

May turned away. "*Yakamashii, kusojijii.*"

"Right. Well, same to you, *momzer.*" Leery turned his back on the cell and grinned at Dru. "He's upset."

"I gathered," she said. "I wonder what the lieu's 'suitable welcome' is."

"You and me, both. She's got a wicked streak when it comes to things like this."

"Yeah," said Dru in a wry tone. "I seem to remember."

"Right." Leery pulled out his chair and sank into it with a sigh. "Speaking of that, did you two get everything worked out?"

"I think so. I'm going to kill my parents, and she agreed not to arrest me."

"Sounds like my kind of plan. Are you sure it will work?"

Dru flashed a wry grin at him. "You know my father's undead, right?"

"Yeah, and I bet your mother has more than a few tricks up her sleeve."

"That she does. And Abaddon owes her about a thousand favors. On second thought, *you* try to kill them while I hide."

Leery grinned. "Sounds like a fun evening. Too bad I have Yankees tickets."

"It's not baseball season, Leery."

"Right. I meant Knicks tickets."

"Ah. You know they are playing away, right?"

"Sure, sure. I've got plane tickets, too." He grinned at her. "Uh, where are they playing tonight?"

"Miami."

"Ah, good. I can work on my shuffleboard technique in the morning."

20

Van Helsing appeared at Leery's desk two hours later. "Come with me, Toto. I need you to carry something."

"Sometimes a guy gets the feeling he's only appreciated for his strong back," said Oriscoe, getting to his feet. "Do I need my coat?"

"Nah. We'll meet the Instacart driver at the elevators."

"Instacart, huh? You're getting all techie, Lieu."

"Perish the thought, Leery. But it *is* convenient for a ghost."

They walked to the elevator—well, Leery walked and Epatha floated along like his balloon. Leery pressed the button to take them to the first floor, casting a surreptitious glance at Van Helsing.

"So... Dru says you two worked things out."

"We did," said Van Helsing with a curt nod. "She's going to talk to her parents."

"Right. She asked me to help with that, but I've got Knicks tickets."

"They're away tonight."

"Does everyone know these things but me?" Leery muttered.

"Evidently." Epatha grinned at him.

"What's the plan for the asshole in the holding cell?"

"I had the impression you liked the asshole in holding."

Leery nodded. "Yeah, but that was before he cursed at me in Japanese."

"How rude."

"Yep. I had to look it up on the computer. First, he called me a coward and told me to drop dead. Then, he called me an old fart and told me to shut up."

"Oh, the horror."

"And that was *after* I told him names could never hurt me." Leery grinned, and Epatha chuckled. "Twice in one day, Lieu. You're going to ruin your reputation as a hardcase if you keep laughing like a giddy schoolgirl."

"Shut up, Benji."

"Hinton already used that one today. You two need to get some kind of system going."

"Clifford, then."

"That's better. I always liked the color red." The elevator doors slid open with a low grinding sound. Outside, stood a guy in a lime green shirt. "He's here, Lieu," Leery murmured. Van Helsing disappeared, as Oriscoe stepped out of the elevator car. "You the Instacart driver?"

"Yep. Order for Van Helsing?"

"Right." Leery reached into his pocket and pulled out a few bills.

"Thanks, but the tip was included."

"Oh. Fine."

"So... I've got to ask, man."

"What's that, champ?"

"Is this some kind of a joke? Van Helsing?"

"Nope, no joke. That's my lieutenant's name."

"Like in Dracula?"

"Nah. Well, same name, but her family just happens to be lucky like that. Dracula is fiction, anyway."

"Oh, no. It was based on this guy named Vlad the Impaler, who—"

"Yeah, thanks, but I've got to get back to work."

"Sorry." He handed two brown paper bags to Leery. "Here's the order."

"Right. Have a good day."

As he stepped back into the elevator, he peeked in the bags. They were filled with bags of dried beans and cartons of eggs. "Are we cooking him lunch, Lieu?"

"Just wait, Oriscoe. Just you wait." She reappeared as the elevator doors slid shut. "Nice cover, by the way."

"If only that poor sap knew the true story behind Dracula."

"Or the Van Helsing clan," she said.

"Right. Or that."

They re-entered the squad room, and Epatha beelined for the holding cell. "Over here, Nogan," she called. "Bring that stuff, Leery."

The three gathered around the holding cell door, and John May eyed them with frank suspicion. "What's this?" he asked no one in particular.

"My detectives tell me you need a little encouragement. Tell us why Lothidn really left the fight circuit."

May scoffed and sneered at Van Helsing. "*Fuzakeruna, abazure.*"

"Muck-spout." Van Helsing arched an eyebrow and turned to Leery. "Start with the dry goods. I'm as much a podsnapper as anyone else, but batty-fang this bobolyne."

"Uh, sure, Lieu... Whatever you say."

She gestured at the bag, then lifted her hand toward May. "Have at him."

Leery set the bags at his feet and withdrew two bags of dried beans, handing one to Dru. "Uh, what do we do with them, Lieu?"

Van Helsing inclined her head and rubbed her eyes. "*Throw* them, Leery. At him."

Leery shrugged and threw the package of dried beans at the cell door, where it slid to the floor with a thump.

"No, harecop. Throw *beans* at him, not the package."

"Okay." Leery retrieved his package and split it along the top. He reached in grabbed a handful. "One at a time or?"

"Handfuls will work."

Leery scanned May's grimacing face and shrugged. He cocked his hand back and let the beans fly. May grunted with each bean that struck him and raised his hands to cover his face.

"Now, *Shuten-doji*," said Van Helsing. "We can do this all day, but if you answer our questions..."

May turned his back.

"Again, Leery. You too, Nogan."

Oriscoe and Nogan began pelting May with handfuls of dried beans, and he reacted as though it were buckshot, twitching and jerking. They continued throwing beans, and he took small steps toward the back of the cell, grunting and gasping.

"Had enough?" asked Van Helsing.

"This is *torture*," said May. "Nothing I say will be admissible!"

"Oh, you're a magister? Sorry, I didn't know." Leery cocked his hand back.

"Wait! Just wait."

"We're listening," said the lieutenant.

"I already told them," said May. "Lothidn got a better job—one where he wouldn't have to bleed for his pay."

"Uh-huh. He'd just make other people bleed, right?"

"I don't know anything else."

"Don't sell me a dog, *Shuten-doji*. I can smell your lies," said Van Helsing.

"It's—"

"Leery."

Oriscoe let his handful of beans fly, and they slapped into May, driving him to his knees.

"Stop!"

"Then speak the truth, son of Oni."

"Okay! Okay... A bugge came to see him—ugly son of a bitch. He wanted Lothidn to, uh, perform *surgery* on a few mundanes. Said there was a market for certain parts—"

"Arms," said Leery.

May nodded. "Sure. Arms. He said there was a back order or something. Lothidn was keen, so..." He hunched his shoulders in a shrug.

"Right. How do you know all this?"

"The bugge came to my shop."

"And what was his name? This bugge?"

"Deermaid. Something like that."

"Diarmaid?" said Leery, pronouncing it 'deer-mid.'

"Yeah, that's it."

"This bugge give you a last name?"

May grimaced and wagged his head side to the side. "I really don't want to get involved, Oriscoe. The Unseelie Court is..."

Leery rustled the beans left in his package.

May held up his hands. "O'Dublin."

Leery nodded as if he'd expected it. "Fine." He glanced at Van Helsing. "Diarmaid O'Duibhne."

"See?" she said to May. "That wasn't so hard, was it?" She cocked her head and squinted at the demon-spawn. "But there's more to it, isn't there."

"No, nothing," said May, staring her in the eye.

"Oh, I think there is. Let's stop all this balming." She gestured at the bag. "We've also got eggs. Three hundred sixty of them."

May blanched, and he backed up until the bench at the rear of the cell hit the back of his legs. "No…"

"Yes," said Epatha with a terse nod. "And I know how to use them."

"At least one of us does," muttered Leery.

"Out with it, *Shuten-doji. All* of it."

He dropped his gaze and stared at the floor, shoulders hunched. "I need protection."

"Protection? From who?"

"Not who. What," he said in a weary voice.

Epatha shot a glance at Leery and lifted her eyebrows.

Leery leaned against his desk and set the bag of beans down. "The Unseelie Court brokering the work?"

"Right," said May after heaving a sigh.

"For someone that scares even the son of a demon?"

May lifted his palm toward Leery and let it drop.

"Who?" asked Epatha.

"The Zombie mafia, if my guess is right."

Inside the cell, May slumped against the back wall. "I'm not saying another word without a deal for protection."

Van Helsing nodded to herself. "I'll go call the LM's office."

21

Angie Carmichael strode into Van Helsing's office. She wore a light gray suit embroidered with runes in silver thread. "What's the emergency?"

"Did you see that devil in our holding tank?" asked Van Helsing.

"The Nephilim? What about him?"

"He's no angel," said Leery. "That's *Shuten-doji*, in the flesh."

Angie raised her eyebrows. "Really?"

"Really."

"What's he doing in New York?"

Leery lifted both hands to either side of his face and made quote-fingers. "Turning over a new leaf. Re-inventing himself as an illegal fight promoter and meat packing plant operator."

"*Meat packing*?"

"To be honest, there's never any meat there. That's pretty much a front for his fighting ring."

Carmichael smirked. "So not so much re-invention going on."

"Not so you'd notice. He's been my CI for a few years, though. Decent information—most of the time. We had to get creative this time, though. He's scared."

"Scared of what? He's the child of an Oni, isn't he?"

Leery nodded. "Scared of the zombies."

She put her hand on her hip, tilting her head to one side. "Zombies."

"*Noster Est.*"

"You've got to be kidding." She turned her gaze on Van Helsing, who spread her translucent hands wide. "The Zombie mafia."

"That's what the man says," said Leery. "He wants protection."

"Right." Angie peeked out the door at May. "And what does he have to trade?"

"Information on an arms dealing ring."

"What kind of weapons are we talking about."

"No, no. You misunderstood," said Epatha. "They are dealing *arms*, not weapons."

"That's sick!"

"No argument here."

Angie sighed. "Fine. Get him in an interview room where we can talk to him in private, and let's see what he has to say."

Ten minutes later, Leery brought May into the interview room where Angie was seated next to Dru. He pointed at the empty chair and went to perch on the windowsill. "John, meet Angie Carmichael, Assistant Locus Magister. Angie, meet John."

"*Shuten-doji*, you mean."

May grimaced. "I'm trying to leave all that behind me."

"Indeed. And running an illegal fight operation where you no doubt drink the blood of the wounded is how you chose to start?"

"We don't all have silver spoons in our mouths."

"Silver spoon? Ha! You don't know anything about me, demon-spawn."

"Likewise, witch."

"Ah, but that's where you're wrong. I know all about the exploits of *Shuten-doji*."

"In *Japan*, maybe. That was a century ago."

"Tell me, Oriscoe," said Angie. "How many unsolved abductions of women are there in the Locus of New York?"

"Mundanes, supers, or both?"

"Take your pick."

Leery turned his gaze on May. "A lot."

Angie held up her hand toward Leery. "There you go. Wasn't that your MO back in Japan, *Shuten-doji*?"

"I don't use that name anymore," said May in a petulant voice.

"Right. *May*, then. Have you gotten up to your old tricks in this locus? Kidnapped women and drank their blood?"

"No. I... I made other arrangements."

"And did your fighters know about those arrangements?"

May crossed his arms and slumped. "Do you want my information or not?"

Angie sighed. "What do you know?"

"I'm not telling you without a deal. I want immunity and protection. A new name, new locus, new job, the works."

"You want an awful lot for a demon hiding behind a mask."

May shrugged without looking at her.

"How am I supposed to know your information is worth the price?"

"It's about the zombies. About occult cabals."

"So I'm told." Angie sucked her teeth. "We can talk about protection, but transactional immunity? No way."

"I'm not going to jail over this farce."

"Keep hard balling me and I promise you, you will."

May turned his gaze on Leery. "Tell her how I've helped you in other cases."

"Already did, pal," said Leery in a quiet voice. "You've got to sing for your supper here."

John inclined his head, then peeked at Angie. "I want a deal in exchange for information about the zombie body parts operation. I'll name names of bosses in *Noster Est*. I'll give you addresses of processing plants; I'll tell you how to find the dealers. I'll give you Lothidn and Diarmaid O'Duibhne. Whatever you want. What's that worth to you?"

"Which bosses?"

"Rose Marie Van Dee, for a start."

Angie sat up straight in her chair and looked at Leery, one eyebrow lifted.

"Got me, counselor. I didn't know he reached such lofty heights."

A smug smile stretched across May's lips. "So, we were talking about immunity?"

22

Angie came back to Van Helsing's office. "Okay, Epatha. The deal's signed, but he better come through, or I'll tie him to the stake myself."

"Oh, he'll talk."

Carmichael nodded. "I saw the beans on the floor." She clicked her teeth. "Risky."

Epatha smiled and spread her hands. "We thought he was hungry."

Angie held her hand out. "Don't tell me. It's better I don't know."

"Is he giving Leery and Dru the information?"

"Yeah." Angie glanced at her watch. "I've got to get back. Let me know if he's full of crap."

"Will do."

23

Leery and Dru stood against the wall in the corridor of a seedy three-floor walk-up, arrayed behind the same SWAT team they'd used to bring Lothidn in. Nogan's face wore a sour, pained expression, but Leery smiled enough for both of them anyway. "Same as last time?" he asked.

One of the servitor warriors spun in a slow circle. "Yes," he said in bell-like tones. "Stay back. Let us do our jobs."

"Let's take the alley, Oriscoe," said Dru. "At least then we might *help*."

"Out there in the cold?"

"I'm going," she said and turned toward the stairs.

Leery turned back to the SWAT officer. "I guess we'll be in the alley."

"Suit yourself."

"We want everyone—dealers, buyers, guards, cockroaches. *Everyone*."

"Yes, the briefing made that clear."

"And if you come across Lothidn—"

"Yes, yes!"

Leery nodded and followed Dru down the stairs. "Couldn't have suggested the alley before we climbed up three flights?"

"Exercise, Oriscoe. Ever hear of it?"

"Elevators, Nogan. Ever hear of them?"

They reached the ground floor and snaked their way back to the alley behind the building. A fire escape hung by rusty bolts from the brick wall, missing its ladder from the first-floor landing to the ground.

The wind howled down the alley, ruffling Leery's hair. "Hope you're happy, Princess," he muttered.

"Not especially. I don't like standing around."

"Adrenaline junky." Leery tsked and shook his head. "Dangerous habit on this job."

"No, it's not that. All my life, servants have taken care of anything distasteful in our household. Disposing of the bodies of Daddy's victims. Cleaning out Mommy's bedroom after her supper. I was...*shielded* from everything that might upset me. *Protected*. Coddled."

"Sounds rough."

"Yeah, as a matter of fact, it *was*, Oriscoe," said Dru with some heat in her voice. "Oh, not then; I didn't know any better. The point is, all those servants, those people who were more like family than my parents, those people *suffered* in my stead. When I was sixteen, and I realized it, I swore to never again let someone take my place in something nasty."

"Well, in this case, Dru, no one is standing in for you. Those therianthropes upstairs knew what they were getting into when they signed up. Hell, they probably *want* the action. And the servitor warriors? Their wizard counterparts are safe and sound in the C3. No, you've got it backward. If we horned our way in, *we'd* be the ones standing in for *them*."

Dru crossed her arms and looked down at the bricks lining the garbage-strewn alley. "What's the C3?"

"Command, Control, and Communications. That tractor-trailer out front with SWAT all over the side."

"Oh."

They both paused and looked up as a window shattered on the third floor. A red and white cooler flew out the window and bounced off the opposite wall of the alley, cracking along one corner and tumbling into an open dumpster. The Ganeshan trumpeted inside the apartment, and the sound of wood splintering and glass shattering followed it.

"Heads up," said Leery.

Dru wrote runes in the air that glowed with pent up energy. She connected them with a ten-pointed star and stood ready to invoke the figure's power.

Leery backed up until his shoulders pressed against the cold, rough bricks of the building behind. His gaze locked on the shattered window, and as another cooler came flying out, he motioned for Dru to step back.

The cooler struck the grimy alley floor and shattered, spilling human arms into the other refuse with the wet splat of rotten tomatoes. Dru curled her lip, but Leery never even glanced at it.

Upstairs, a werewolf howled, and Leery threw back his head and howled back, eyes glowing with chartreuse light. "Be ready," he growled. "That was a warning from our boy upstairs."

The unmistakable sound of automatic gunfire erupted from the apartment, followed by the pained shriek of the Garudan. Power exploded from inside, shattering the rest of the apartment's windows and raining yet more glass down on them.

A zombie dove out onto the fire escape and tumbled down the stairs to the second floor, grunting each time she struck a new step. She rolled to her hands and knees and shucked for the next flight without bothering to get up. Her skin was black and curled away from exposed patches of bone and decaying flesh.

Another zombie crashed through the window, moving at a full sprint and sailing right over the edge of the fire escape. He fell to the alleyway with a scream and hit the bricks with the dry-kindling sound of shattering bone.

"Stay down, buddy," grunted Leery, his gaze locked on the zombie coming down to the first-floor fire escape. "You're busted—literally."

The zombie looked down at his shattered legs and groaned. "Very funny."

The other zombie paused and glared at Dru, then turned her gaze on Leery. "Oriscoe?"

"Christ, is that Dee Terry? What have you gotten yourself into?"

She stood there on the fire escape, her gaze switching to the broken zombie. "Ah, Jack. You're busted."

"In more ways than one," said Leery. "Come down from there, Dee. Both of you are under arrest."

Magical fire flamed out the windows of the apartment upstairs, and a bugge holding an AK-47 flipped over the windowsill and onto the metal grate of the fire escape. He landed with a sickening thump but kept hold of the gun.

"Dru," said Leery.

The bugge rolled to one knee and glared downward. He got his short legs underneath him and stood, his head coming to just above the height of the railing. His thin, greasy hair hung in his eyes, and he brushed it aside with a long-fingered, pus-riddled hand. His pale-yellow eyes flashed on Leery for a moment before settling on Dru. He lifted the rifle to his shoulder and squeezed the trigger.

Dru mumbled a power word and flung her spell upward. At the same moment, Dee cast herself over the railing of the first-floor fire escape and crashed into a row of garbage cans.

The spell slammed the bugge into the wall behind him, shimmering and flashing where it contacted his pasty flesh. He screamed and cursed at them, thrashing side-to-side, the AK-47 cartwheeling through the air to land butt-first on the ground next to Jack.

The zombie lunged at it, sweeping it up like a mother hugging a sick child to her breast.

"Let 'em have it, Jack," said Dee.

"Dee Terry!" snapped Leery. "What would your mother say?"

"Who cares?" said Dee. "She's gone, and I'm still living...well, sort of."

The zombie named Jack sat up, grimacing at the mess of his own legs, and shouldered the AK-47.

Before he could pick a target, Leery's eyes blazed with yellow-green light and his clothes split down the middle and fell away. Even as his body contorted into werewolf form, he leaped at the zombie, arms thrown wide, mouth open and snarling.

The zombie, sitting straight up, turned the rifle on him and pulled the trigger. A stream of bullets exploded from the gun's barrel, but with each round, the barrel moved up and to the right from the recoil, and most of the slugs slammed into the brick wall to Leery's left.

Even so, four rounds slammed into Leery's torso and he howled, his lip curling back in rage. He struck the rifle away and bowled the broken zombie over, sinking his fangs into the dead flesh of the zombie's arm.

"Jack!" screamed Dee as she sprang out of the jumble of garbage cans. She ran forward and kicked Leery in the back.

He snarled and shook his head back and forth. With a sickening pop, Jack's forearm tore away from his elbow, and the zombie flopped to the side with a groan.

"Shit!" Jack yelled. "I'm falling apart!"

Leery flung the forearm away and whirled to his feet, facing Dee, lips curled back from his fangs, a low, prey-freezing growl rumbling in his chest. She backed away as he advanced on her slowly, arms thrown wide, neck hunched toward her, ears flattened against his skull.

Dru wrote runes in the air. Glaring at Dee, she shouted two words in the *Verba Patiendi*, and the zombie woman shrieked and wrapped her arms around her chest, squeezing herself tight. She backed away from Leery and pressed herself into the brick wall behind her. He snarled and turned his back on her, glowering at Jack where he lay.

Another burst of power thrummed from within the apartment on the third floor, and the bugge screeched as it shuddered through him. He writhed against Dru's spell and began to sing, his sweet, pure voice filling the alley like smoke, overriding the noise from the apartment, the street sounds coming from the mouth of the alley.

Leery's ears twitched, then oriented upward. Dru's gaze snapped to the bugge, going wide. She sketched four runes in the air and connected them with two perpendicular slashes. She shouted a word of power and flung the spell at Leery, who had already started running toward the fire escape.

He snapped his head toward her, eyes blazing, and roared at her. His eyes rolled in their sockets and saliva drooped from his lips. He staggered sideways, grabbing his skull.

Jack dragged himself toward the mouth of the alley using his remaining limb, and Dee stumbled after him. The bugge peeled himself away from the wall and hurled himself down the stairs toward the second-floor landing. He smashed his hand through the window and flung himself through the broken pane. Once inside the apartment, he stopped singing.

Leery shook his head, looked at Dru with wide eyes, and nodded. She pointed toward the mouth of the alley. He spun and charged after the zombies, and Dru followed.

24

Leery stood in a corner inside one of the Command, Control, and Communications meeting rooms, wrapped in a blanket, sipping from a huge mug of steaming coffee, and glared at Dee Terry. Dru leaned across the stainless-steel table and put her finger in the zombie's face.

"You'd better figure this out, and fast," Dru snarled. "You're in a heap of shit here, Terry."

"Where is Jack? What have you done to him?"

"Dee, you've got a lot more to worry about than where your undead boyfriend is. Wise up, woman, and start cooperating, or we'll slap you into the dungeon and let you rot."

"Literally," said Dru with a sneer.

"But—"

"No buts, Dee. You're only getting this chance because our mothers were friends back in the day."

The zombie woman dropped her gaze to her lap. "Is he okay? Tell me that much."

"You saw the state he was in." Leery shrugged and stepped out of the corner. "The good news is that he's already dead and can't die again."

"That's where you're wrong, Oriscoe. If he gets chopped up enough, he'll get lost, and if that happens, he'll never be the same." She glanced at him, then cut her eyes away. "That's how she punishes zombies who displease her. She grinds them up and spreads their parts across five states."

"Who, Dee?"

"You know who!" she snapped, slamming her hand into the table.

"Right, Dee. We already know who you mean, but if you don't say it, we can't help you. If you don't help us, I don't *want* to help you." Leery slurped his coffee and peered at her over its top.

She slumped and heaved a sigh—which everyone in the room realized was only for effect. She needed to breathe about as much as Dru needed to eat meat. "What do you want to know?" she asked in a dead voice.

"Start with the name," said Dru.

"Fine, but I need protection. And protection for Jack, too."

"I'll do what can be done on your behalf, but only if you talk." Leery tightened his grip on the blanket. "Now."

She stared at him, her mouth twisted in a sneer. "Fine. Rose Marie Van Dee. Happy now?"

"Far from it. How did you get hooked up with the Van Dee cabal? You came from good people."

"Did I?" she sneered and leaned forward. "Then, when I died and awoke like this, where did they go? They *shunned* me, Leery. I haven't spoken to anyone in years, because *they don't want anything to do with me.*"

"And you turned to the Zombie Mob to teach them a lesson? You know they're not really a family, right?"

"Duh, werewolf. *Jack* is my family, now."

"Jack who?" asked Dru.

"Jack Barnett."

"And what ties does he have with the Van Dees?"

"He's nothing but a soldier. Like me."

"You sure about that?" asked Dru in a quiet voice.

Dee shrugged. "What else?"

"Maybe a street lieutenant?"

The zombie blew a raspberry. "Yeah, sure."

"Hey, somebody was in charge of that apartment. Are you trying to tell us it was you?"

"The bugge."

"Nah. That doesn't track, Dee." Leery pulled out the chair opposite from her and sat. "Keep that up, and I'll bury you in the dungeon and forget you are there."

She rolled her eyes, and the dry, raspy sound it made sickened Dru. "Come on, Dee. You don't owe Rose Marie a single thing."

"I *know* that! But she will grind me to hamburger and distribute my molecules to hell and back."

"That's why you want protection, right? You have to give something to get something." Dru stood and took Leery's spot in the corner.

"You owe me that much, Dee. You and your buddy cost me a set of clothes, a great camel hair coat, and the most comfortable pair of shoes I've ever owned."

The zombie made a face and looked down at her lap. "Sorry," she said. "You weren't supposed to be back there."

"What's that mean?"

"So, get the LM in here, so I can sign whatever I need to sign and start singing."

"Hold up. What did you mean, we weren't supposed to be there?"

Dee turned her face away. "The hallway."

"What about the hallway."

"You were supposed to wait in the hall. The alley should have been empty."

Leery turned to look at Dru. "Why do you say that, Dee?"

"Get the LM. I'll tell you everything, then."

"Fine."

25

Angie shivered and pulled her coat tighter against the wind. She climbed up the folding metal steps, and as she reached the top, Leery opened the door, his blanket flapping in the wind. "Uh, am I interrupting something?" she asked with a grin.

Leery stood in the doorway, blocking her path. "Had to split my clothes. Zombies." He rolled his eyes skyward. "Hey, before you come in. I know this woman—or I knew her when she was a living, breathing woman. We grew up together."

"Is it a problem?"

"No, not that. But listen, she's made an allegation. Or at least noises that sound like an allegation."

"About?"

"About a mole in the SWAT team. Or maybe at One Police Plaza."

Angie grimaced. "Tell me."

"Dru and I went down to cover the alley. That's how we caught Dee and her little friend, Jack Barnett. She says we weren't supposed to be there, that we should have been in the hallway."

"And who told her that?"

"She wouldn't say until she had a deal."

"A sentencing deal?"

"And one for protective custody."

Angie puffed out her cheeks. "How many protection deals do we need to give out in this case?"

Leery stepped back. "I don't know, counselor. One for every supernatural crook in Manhattan?"

"The Dark Queen forbid."

"Don't let Dru hear you say that. She's sensitive." Leery grinned and stepped back, ushering Angie inside.

26

Dru stood in the corner, arms crossed over her breasts, glowering at Dee Terry over Angie and Leery's heads. The zombie wouldn't look at her and seemed to have a hard time meeting Angie's gaze, either.

"That's not how this works, Ms. Terry. You have to take it on faith that I will draw up the papers and get them to your magister for his review. It's not like on television. I don't carry blank agreements around in my briefcase ready to have your name penned into it at a moment's notice."

"But if I tell you anything, someone in the Van Dee family will get to me—"

"Yes, I understand you need protection, Ms. Terry. I've heard your reasoning, and I agree with you. I will get you your deal, but we need your information now."

"Dee," said Leery. "She's not pulling a fast one. This is how it works."

Dee heaved another sigh.

"Yes, we know you're frustrated," said Angie. "We also know you don't need to breathe."

"Right. But the undead girl has to take everything on faith. You hold all the cards, and I have to talk before you'll play them."

"Anyone who wants a deal speaks first." Angie shrugged and shoved her legal pad into her bag. "But if you're not interested..."

"Okay, okay. But you're my witness, Oriscoe. You better back me up if she refuses to follow through."

Leery drew a deep breath. "She won't do that, Dee. Not unless you lie or withhold information."

"Right. So, yes, I'm a member of the Van Dee Cabal. I'm a soldier, and so is Jack."

"Yeah, we heard that before," said Dru. "Fast forward to the part where you give us *useful* information."

Dee sneered at her and narrowed her eyes. "Ask me what you want to know, then."

"Come on, Dee," said Oriscoe. "Tell us who leaked the raid."

The zombie shrugged. "I'm not sure who leaked it, just that we got a call that you were on the way. We were supposed to leave before you arrived, but Jack wanted to take the merchandise, and we needed to get it packed for transport." She glanced at Leery. "We were told the alley was our escape route."

"Who was in charge in the apartment?"

"Well, Jack was if no one higher up in the family was around." She scoffed. "Which means he was in charge all the time."

Leery glanced at Angie and raised his eyebrows. She waved him on. "Then who did Jack report to? You know, while no one else was around."

"A guy in Long Island City. He had a butcher's shop or something."

"I'll kill him," muttered Leery.

"I take it that's *Shuten-doji*?" asked Angie in a voice dripping with acid.

"Got it in one. Tell me his paperwork hasn't gone through, yet."

"The ink isn't even dry." Angie waved her hand at Dee Terry. "What else?"

"How does John Michael May fit in Rose Marie Van Dee's organization?" asked Leery, leaning across the table toward Dee Terry.

"The guy in the butcher's shop?"

"Yes."

"He's got ties to Van Dee, but he's not a zombie, so..."

"Right. He's not dead, so he can't have his badge."

"Yeah, that's right," said Dee. "He's got special status, though, because he's higher up than a lot of other zombies I know."

"We're going to want you to lay out the structure of the Van Dee family," said Angie. "While you're doing that, make sure you mark any non-zombies with ties to Van Dee."

Dee turned her head to the side and shrugged with one shoulder. "Whatever. It won't matter."

"And why's that, Dee?" asked Leery.

"Because she will—"

"She's lying," said Dru.

Angie half-turned in her chair and glanced back at Dru. "About what?"

"Most of it, I think. Not about *Shuten-doji*, he's definitely in deeper than he let on, but this nonsense about Jack..."

"Shut your damn mouth!" snapped Dee.

"And she's not just some soldier following orders, either."

Dee narrowed her eyes and crossed her arms over her chest. "Think I'm lying? Prove it."

Dru snorted a laugh. "I'm enchanted, dead-girl. Soothsayer rune set. Ever hear of it?"

"Screw off, you demon bitch," muttered Dee.

"Listen, if you're going to yank our chains, I'll ship you off right now, Ms. Terry. I'll include a note in your sheet that you're *never* to have contact with this Jack..." She glanced at Leery and beckoned.

"Jack..." Leery bent and grabbed a loose stack of papers from the floor and rifled through them. "Ah. Here it is. Jackson Barnett."

Angie nodded and turned a brutal gaze on Dee. "I'll make sure you have zero contact with Jackson Barnett. *And*, I'll make sure you are put in lockdown." She smiled, and it seemed as if the temperature in the room dropped twenty degrees. "Think of that deep, dark hole as the grave you evaded, because I'll *bury you in it.*"

Silence fell over them. In the main room outside the door, one of the wizards running a servitor warrior laughed, and the other joined him a moment later. Someone opened the outside door and let it slam in the wind behind them.

"So. Ms. Terry, what's it going to be?" asked Angie. "I'll give you ten seconds to consider your options. And while you're doing that, get this through your jellified brain: if you lie to me again, I won't care what kind of information you promise me, I'll bury you as deep in the dungeons of this Locus as I can, and I'll come to every single one of your parole hearings—if you ever get any, which I doubt, because Sam McCoy will listen when I tell him how you've lied, and he will go for your throat like a bulldog."

"And they don't call him the Stakeman for nothing, Dee," said Leery. "Hell, I wouldn't put it past him to make it his personal mission to get burnings reinstated."

Angie nodded. "He doesn't quit, Ms. Terry. Ever. So, what's your choice? Do I call for transport to Rikers?"

Dee's gaze bounced back and forth between them, then darted back at Dru. "Fine," she said with a sigh. "But Jack needs protection, too. Bring him to me and make him part of the deal. Together, we'll tell you everything we know, but you have to give us new identities in another Locus."

Angie wagged her head to the side. "I'll see what we can do."

Dee shook her head. "Not good enough."

Angie scoffed. "Do I have to repeat that speech I just made? That's disappointing"—

she glanced at Leery—"I thought it was so good."

"Oh, it was, counselor. It was."

"Then bury me!" snapped Dee. "I'm not going to say another word until the ink is dry on the plea deal."

Angie stood and chuckled. "Leery?"

"Yes, counselor?"

"Call Rikers and reserve a pit for Ms. Terry. I'll get the paperwork for her *interment* started."

"Please," whispered Dee. "I'll give you everything... I'll give you Rose Marie Van Dee herself. On a platter..."

Angie stopped packing her briefcase. "What do you have on her?"

"Enough," sighed Dee. "I'll give you enough so that you can do to her all the things you just threatened to do to me."

Angie pursed her perfect lips and glanced at Leery.

"Hey, I just work here." He grinned. "But Rose Marie Van Dee? Burying her in a deep pit will cripple the Zombie mafia for years."

Angie pinched the bridge of her nose and sighed. "Yeah. I suppose you're right." She glowered at Dee. "If you're lying to me—"

"Yeah, yeah. Dark pit. Interment. Yeah, I get it, counselor."

Angie looked to Dru and raised an eyebrow.

"She believes what she's saying."

"Fine, Ms. Terry. I'll make your deal."

CHAPTER 3

THE COURT CASE

I

Sam McCoy came out of his office like a charging bull, slamming his door against the wall as he did so. "Angie! What the hell is this?"

Wearing a lopsided grin, Angie pushed herself away from her desk and stood. "What I had to do to get the information."

"This is a sweetheart of a deal! Transactional immunity? Those two zombies won't get any time at all."

"I know, Sam. But they're giving us something major in return."

"Well, don't keep me in suspense. What did they promise?"

Angie pursed her lips and glanced to either side. "It's not so much what as who, but we shouldn't speak of it out here."

"Enough with the cloak and dagger, Angie," Sam said, his craggy brows slamming together.

"In your office?"

Sam shook his head and sucked his teeth, then whirled without another word and returned to his office. Angie followed him inside and closed the door behind her.

"What's all this about, Angie?" he asked as he walked toward his desk.

"It's about Rose Marie Van Dee. It's about *Shuten-doji*. It's about the Unseelie Court."

Sam stopped for a moment, then continued to his chair and sank into it. "Credible?"

"I think so."

"Spill it, then."

"Oriscoe and Nogan—"

"*Nogan*," Sam scoffed.

"Oriscoe and Nogan caught a case where two mundanes were murdered. It led them to a zombie chop shop, and we caught two zombies, a bugge, and...*Shuten-doji*."

Sam raised his eyebrows.

"There's at least one more who's still in the wind—a Norwegian Wood Troll—but Leery says they're closing in on him."

"And Van Dee is tied directly to this chop shop?"

"No, but we turned the two zombies." She dimpled. "They're in love."

Sam raised his eyebrows again and shook his head.

"They can give us Van Dee on several counts of murder-for-hire, not to mention commissioning the murders of mundanes for their body parts."

Sam looked down at the agreement in his hands, set it on the desk in front of him, and signed his name on it. "All I can say is, these zombie lovers had better come through."

"Trust me, Sam. We've already explained how I will bury her in the darkest pit I can find while you fight to bring back stake burnings." Angie hit him with her most stunning smile.

"Make sure her information is good," said Sam without smiling. "I want you to prep her until she can give her testimony in her sleep."

"You got it, boss."

"And invite Rose Marie Van Dee to spend some time at the resort on Rikers Island."

2

Leery leaned back in the easy chair, his gaze bouncing back and forth between Jack Barnett and Dee Terry as they flirted and pretended to argue—which was another way to flirt as far as he could tell. He rubbed his eyes with his thumb and forefinger, not quite suppressing the sigh that kicked the back of his teeth.

"Oh, I'm sorry, wolfman," said Jack. "Are we *bothering* you?"

"Hey, I'd tell you to get a room, but...well..." He smirked and waved his hand at the cheap motel room's decor.

"You don't have to stay in here with us, Leery," said Dee. "It's not like we dare step one foot outside that door. Even if this place *is* a dump."

"Your tax dollars at work." Leery stood and walked to the window, peeking out from behind the blinds. "I really hate sitting around."

"Me, too," said Jack, grimacing down at the wheelchair he sat in and waving his remaining hand at the space where his legs used to be. "Is the Locus going to come through with new parts to replace the ones you ruined, wolfman?"

"Hey, I had nothing to do with your legs. That was your own stupidity. And as for the arm, I would've left it alone if not for that AK-47. You're lucky I left the bit above the elbow."

Jack sneered and made a noise deep in his throat.

A knock sounded, and Leery walked over to the door and peered through the peephole. "Time to go to work, you two," he said. He opened the door and let Angie Carmichael in. "Counselor," he said.

"How are the fleas, Oriscoe?" she asked with a saucy grin.

"Oh, you know, complaining about the room. Yammering about who's going to replace the body parts lost during the raid." He glanced at Jack and grinned.

"Right," said Angie. "But I meant—"

"How long do we have to babysit these two?" Leery asked. "I think they'd rather be alone."

"Well, you—and they—will have to suffer through. In silence, I hope."

Nodding and smiling, Leery turned back to the window. "You didn't see Nogan out there, did you?"

"No. Why?"

"She went for coffee."

"Of course she did." Angie shook her head and rolled her eyes, then turned to the zombies. "Okay, dead things, it's time to work."

"We need to talk about getting me a new arm and some legs. This wheelchair is—"

"The best you're going to get until after the trial."

"But if the Cabal comes after us, I won't—"

"That's why you have NYPD's finest sitting with you," she said. "Now, we need to go over some things, and then we'll go through your testimony."

"Again?" snapped Dee.

"And again. And again, and yet again," said Angie, nodding.

Dee drew a deep breath and heaved a sigh.

"Don't do that on the stand. Everyone knows zombies don't need to breathe except to talk or make melodramatic noises."

Dee rolled her eyes back in her head. "Makes a girl wish for true death," she murmured.

"Let's get this over with," grumped Jack. "If you want me over there, you'll have to push me. You know, because I only have *one arm.*"

"Leery?" said Angie without looking up from arranging her papers.

"Right, get the werewolf to do the manual labor." He walked over and pushed Barnett's chair up to the table. "There. Everyone comfy, now? Christ on a stick!"

"You really do need a coffee, don't you?" asked Angie, quirking her eyebrow and grinning at Leery.

"That or a silver bullet."

Angie chuckled and waved him away. "Dee? You want to join us?"

"No. I'm fine right here." She walked her gaze around the small, foul-smelling room. "It's not like I'm any farther away."

"Suit yourself," Angie said with a shrug. "Let's talk about the chop shop."

Jack groaned. "Again?"

"Yes, again. Now, the reason you decided to hire outside labor—"

"*I* didn't decide anything of the sort," said Jack. "I was happy robbing fresh graves for merchandise. The 'new plan' came down from on high."

"From Van Dee?"

"Who else?"

"What I mean is: did you get the order from Rose Marie, herself, or from an intermediary?"

"From the butcher."

"I'm still not understanding his role in the organization. He's not a zombie, so he can't be a made man, right?"

"Right. He isn't."

"Then how can he give the orders?"

Jack's face twisted with distaste and anger. "She likes her rides warm."

Angie's eyebrows shot up. "Does that mean what I think it means?"

"Yes," said Dee. "She prefers someone with a pulse."

"Don't we all?" asked Leery from the window.

"No," said Jack, twisting his head around to look at Dee.

"Yeah, okay. Back on track, people," said Angie. "But tell me how it works. What is *Shuten-doji's* role in the organization? Is he some kind of street captain?"

"She calls him our last link to the living, but that's bullshit," said Dee. "We all call him 'the boy-toy' behind his back."

"Then he isn't respected?"

Jack scoffed while Dee grunted.

"So we come back to my question. Why is he in charge?"

"Because Mama Rose Marie *said so.* She's not a fan of the old way of doing things."

"Thus murdering the mundanes to beef up our inventory."

"Right. Okay, let's leave that for now. Tell me—" The phone rang, and they all turned to look at it.

Leery walked over and grabbed it. "Hello?" He turned and looked at Angie. "Yeah, here she is, Sam." He held the phone out to her.

She listened for a moment, her eyes growing wide, then she nodded. "I'm on my way. No, Oriscoe and Nogan are on guard duty this afternoon. It's best to leave them here."

Leery groaned and went back to the window.

3

Sam waited for Angie at the unmarked door within the Rikers Island jail that hid the stairway down to the dungeon beneath Rikers Island. He held his briefcase in front of him in a two-handed grip. A small smile teased his lips as she approached.

"Is this for real?" she asked.

"I don't know, but if it is..."

"Yeah," she breathed. "Let's go talk to her. Who's her magister?"

Sam grimaced. "Paul Leibman."

"Isn't that your—"

"Yes," Sam muttered. He turned and pushed through the door and started down the steps, leaving Angie to follow in his footsteps. At the bottom of the steps, Sam moved out into the stone anteroom. He glanced at the smoking torches and grimaced. "Halsey, how long until the dungeon is modernized?"

The elf behind the tall desk opposite the stairwell grimaced. "I'm sure you'd know better than me, magister." He glanced at Angie and wrinkled his nose. "Who?"

"You know who!" snapped Sam. "Now, take us to her and cut the horseshit."

Halsey glared at them a moment, then sniffed and turned away, rattling the keys on the massive ring threaded through his belt. He led them through a warren of hallways and pointed at a door next to a flickering torch. "She awaits you there," he said.

"And is her magister present?" Sam asked.

Halsey looked at him for a few breaths, then turned away without answering and retraced his steps, leaving Sam to shake his head at his back.

"Come on, Sam," said Angie. She opened the door and entered the meeting room. A long oak table bisected the room lengthwise, with stiff-looking straight-backed chairs of the same wood ringing it.

Sam came in behind her and walked to a chair across from a silver-haired man in old-fashioned magister robes. "Paul," he said with a nod.

"Sam. I haven't seen you in a long time."

"No, not since you took up defending the Zombie mafia."

The zombie seated next to Paul Leibman snorted and rolled her eyes. "Doesn't everyone deserve a defense?"

Sam ignored her, but Angie met her cool gaze, then scoffed. She pulled out her chair and sat, putting her briefcase on the floor next to her.

"Don't like the undead?" asked Rose Marie Van Dee.

"It's not that," said Angie. "I don't like criminals who invoke the Canon and Covenants when it suits them, while smashing them to bits the rest of the time."

Rose Marie sniffed and shifted her gaze to Sam. "Well, Mr. McCoy? Sit."

Sam tore his eyes away from Leibman's gaze and glared at her. "I don't take orders from you, Rose."

She twitched her head to the side. "I prefer *Rose Marie*. Two words, mind, not Rosemary."

Sam pistoned his shoulders up and down, then pulled out his chair and sank into it. "This had better be good."

"Oh, it is, Sam," said Paul Leibman. "Or at least, it *might* be, if your offer is good enough."

Sam scoffed and shook his head. "You know how this works, Paul. You tell me what you have; I tell you what it's worth."

Paul smiled and shook his head. "Not this time, Sam."

Sam cast a glance at Angie. "Why is it everyone thinks their information is good enough to turn everything on its head?"

Angie snorted.

"No, Paul. Simply, no. If all you have is an empty hook, this old fish ain't biting." He picked up his briefcase and scooted forward in his chair, readying himself to stand. "Now, if you've finished wasting my time, I'll be going."

Paul smiled and waved Sam back. "Relax, Sam. I've got the goods, and you and I both know you want them."

Sam gave him a single shake of his head. "Not sight unseen, I don't."

"Fine. I'll give you a taste, but first, let me tell you where the bidding *starts*." He held up his index finger. "First, Rose Marie does no time. Zero. Second, she gets Witness

Protection, but not the shoe-clerk variety. No, Rose Marie is accustomed to living in a certain style—"

"Let's go, Angie," said Sam. "Next time, Paul, you can give me a request in writing outlining what information your client has, and I'll decide from there whether it's worth talking about." He pushed his chair back with a horrible screech and stood.

Paul's expression darkened, and his smile disappeared. "Now, wait just a minute, McCoy!"

"I don't think so," said Sam.

"Boys, boys," said Rose Marie, holding up her hands.

Angie stared at her left hand, at a flap of loose, rotten skin and the maggot wiggling out from the tear.

Van Dee grimaced and snatched her hand to her lap. "If everyone can stop comparing penises, maybe cooler heads can drive this meeting."

Sam turned a cold glare on her. "Fifteen seconds."

Leibman put his hand on her forearm, but Rose Marie shook it off. She nodded at Sam, a small smile winking from her lips. "Fine, fine.

Law enforcement doesn't know this, but the Cabals are coming together."

"Coming together?" asked Angie. "Not bloody likely."

Rose Marie turned a bored expression on her. "Oh. I forgot. You know everything already." She shifted her gaze back to Sam. "Muzzle your mutt, and I'll go on."

Sam said nothing, but he rested his free hand on Angie's shoulder as she started to come to her feet.

Rose Marie flashed a wicked smile at her. "Good pup!"

"Get on with it!" snapped Sam.

"Yes, well..." Van Dee sniffed.

"Rose Marie, this really isn't—"

"Shut up, Paul," she said in a frigid tone. "As I was saying, the Cabals are coming together, building a super-cabal that spans the Loci. You may have read in the New York Grimoire that I have risen to the top of the heap, so to speak, in this Locus. I floated the idea to several other Cabal leaders, and—"

"This is all very informative, but if this super-cabal was your idea, and I put you in a dungeon somewhere, it will fall apart on its own."

"Are you sure?" Van Dee asked with a grin. "Are you so sure I can't run all this from wherever I am? Are you so sure you can convict me at all?"

Sam shrugged. "One way to find out." He removed his hand from Angie's shoulder, and she shot to her feet.

"Now, just a minute, Sam," said Paul. "I'm sure the Covenancy authorities will be interested—"

"This is my case!" snapped Sam.

Angie smiled sweetly at Rose Marie. "We're going to bury *Rosemary* in a deep pit and hold her *incommunicado*. Let's see what you can run from there."

The only indication of Van Dee's anger was a slight narrowing of her eyes. "You should be careful, dear. In this Locus, you might get hurt after speaking to me like that."

"Is that a threat?" Angie snapped.

"Oh, dear girl, I never make threats." Van Dee smiled, but her eyes remained algid. "I do, however, make *promises* from time to time."

"And there's another charge to add to the complaint, Angie," said Sam. "Assault on a Law Enforcement Officer."

"I'll get that added later today." Angie smiled and winked at Van Dee.

"If I were you, I'd get right to it," said Van Dee. She glowered into Angie's eyes. "Otherwise, you might run out of time to do *anything*."

"Rose Marie," said Leibman. "Stop talking."

"Listen to him, Van Dee," said Sam. "For once, he's giving you good legal advice." He turned and opened the door for Angie, then followed her outside.

4

The next morning, Sam cut through Thomas Paine Park from Lafayette Street, the collar of his coat up, his shoulders hunched against the bitter winter cold. He wore a fedora pulled down to his ears as proof against the barbarous wind. Fat, lazy snowflakes drifted down to perch on the brim of his hat and dust his shoulders. He walked with his head down, eyes scanning the paved path for telltale signs of a broken hip in the form of almost-impossible-to-see ice lurking beneath the slush. As such, he didn't see

Angie until her wordless shout brought his head snapping up.

"Get away from me!" Angie shouted again.

Sam lurched into a fast shuffle, still leery of hidden ice, and raised his hand, ready to cast a spell. "You there!" he shouted at a pack of six burly men blocking her path.

Angie whipped her head around and spotted him, relief clear in her dark eyes. One of the men leaned closer to her and said something that the wind ripped away before Sam could make sense of it, and she recoiled, backing away from the group of men.

As Sam got closer, he realized that each of the men either wore a hoody and dark glasses or had watch caps jammed down over their ears and had their collars turned up. *Zombies*, he thought. *A damn zombie horde*! His gaze darted to the left and the right, hoping to find a cop, but finding no one.

He dropped his briefcase into the snow beside the path and stopped moving forward. Closing his eyes, he concentrated a moment, then chanted a *tempestas maleficium*, calling down a bolt of lightning from the overcast sky and directing it into the zombie's midst and hurling them aside like a toddler's blocks.

Angie threw her hands up around her ears and ducked her face away from the blinding glow but kept moving to his side.

"Are you okay?" Sam asked, not taking his eyes off the zombies lying helter-skelter like fallen bowling pins on the snow surrounding the path.

"They didn't hurt me."

"Stay here." Sam strode forward, cutting the figure of an angry father bent on disciplining his children. "I suppose Van Dee sent you thugs?" he demanded when he reached the zombies lying stunned on the ground. He kicked the nearest one in the leg. "Speak up!"

None of the zombies answered. They could do no more than groan and hold their heads.

"Take this message back to your masters. Come after Angie again, and there'll be hell to pay. Understand me?" He watched them writhe for a moment, then shook his head once. "Bear in mind that I wrote my dissertation on the various forms of execration." He bent and yanked hair from each of the zombies, shoving clumps into his pocket. "If anything happens to Angie, I won't need to see you to ruin you."

Sam turned and made his way back to Angie, retrieving his briefcase as he went. "Let's go before they recover."

"Thank you, Sam."

He pursed his lips and looked at her askance. "Nothing you couldn't have done for yourself." He put his hand on her elbow and guided her down the path, leaving the zombies behind.

They crossed Centre Street and climbed the steps to the courthouse. At the top of the marble steps, Angie turned and looked back toward the park, eyes smoldering, but the zombies were already gone.

"Come, Angie," said Sam in a quiet voice. "We're due in court in five minutes."

She nodded absently and allowed him to turn her and pull her inside.

5

Judge Le Fay took the bench with a flourish and waved her ghostly hand at the gavel. It levitated into the air and banged down. "I call this court to order," she said. She glanced at Angie, but half a heartbeat later, her gaze strayed to McCoy's face. "Ah, ha. We're graced by the presence of the Executive Assistant Locus Magister this morning. To what do we owe the pleasure, Mr. McCoy?"

"Good morning, Your Honor. We're here to arraign a significant thorn in the side of Locus law enforcement."

"Ah ha. And that would be the Mama Zombie?"

"Indeed, Judge Le Fay."

"Very well. I suppose you have a suggestion on bail."

"Yes, Your Honor. The People request remand."

"If it pleases the court, I'm Paul Leibman, Ms. Van Dee's magister. I'd like to point out that my client has never been convicted of a crime, and as such, remand is out of the question."

Le Fay arched an eyebrow at him. "Is it indeed? How strange that I find myself considering the request in solemnity."

"What I mean to say, Your Honor, is that Ms. Van Dee has no record. She has *no convictions*."

"That may be true, Your Honor," said McCoy. "But that has no bearing on the matter. We've charged the defendant with two counts of murder for hire, twenty-seven counts of conspiracy to commit murder for hire, corruption of a law enforcement official—"

"What was the last bit?"

"Corruption of a law enforcement official, Your Honor. At present, we've only leveled one such charge, but it is my frank belief more charges are forthcoming."

"Very well."

"We will also bring charges of bribery, sale of body parts without a license, harvesting body parts without a license, assault against law enforcement officials, improper action, and as of Ms. Carmichael's walk to the courthouse this morning, intimidation of a Locus Magister during commission of her sworn duty."

Le Fay arched an eyebrow and glanced at Leibman. "These charges seem sufficient to warrant remand, Counselor. Don't you agree?"

The defense magister leaned down to allow Van Dee to whisper in his ear. He straightened. "No, Your Honor, and Ms. Van Dee has the means to post bail."

"Your Honor, Ms. Van Dee's organization has already threatened the physical wellbeing of Ms. Carmichael here. If for no other reason than the safety of the court officers involved, I object strongly to any consideration of granting bail. The People also request that her isolation order be carried forward until the conclusion of her trial."

Le Fay looked back and forth between McCoy and Leibman, then waved her hand at her gavel again. The gavel levitated and hovered. "Ms. Van Dee is remanded to the dungeon on Rikers Island and held over for trial. The order of isolation is continued." She snapped her fingers, and the gavel banged down. "Next case!"

6

Sam rapped on Adam's door frame with one knuckle, then stepped inside. The Locus Magister sat behind his impressive desk, reading the newspaper. He glanced over the top of it and treated Sam to a nod.

"We may have problems with this case, Adam."

"Oh? Mob trials are always hard on witnesses. Losing them already?"

"No, it's not that. This morning, six zombies confronted Angie outside the courthouse."

"Is she hurt?"

"No, I came along in time to break it up, but..."

Adam folded his paper and got to his feet. "Call Van Helsing."

"Already done. I just wanted you to know."

"Come with me," said Adam, stepping past Sam into the hall. He walked to Angie's cubicle and smiled down at her as if he were her grandfather. "Sam tells me you had a little excitement this morning."

"No big deal. Sam set things right." She put on a brave face, but her hands shook as she sipped her coffee.

"Yes, I'm sure he did. But a case like this... Things can get dicey. No one would look down on you if you requested a replacement."

"No way." She looked from Adam to Sam and back. "I want to be there when Rose Marie Van Dee gets her comeuppance. I want to look her in the eye and smile as the handcuffs rachet closed and the realization that she'll never walk free again hits her."

"Admirable," said Adam. "But either Mama Zombie or her organization appears to have singled you out for special attention. At the very least, you will accept a protective detail."

"That's not necessary. I—"

"No, you misunderstood me, Angie." Adam spoke at low volume, but his voice rang with iron determination. "You *will* accept a protective detail if you work on this case. We can't count on serendipity to protect you."

Angie opened her mouth, but Sam held up a hand to stop her.

"Listen to him, Angie. Take the detail. I don't have time to train a replacement before the trial."

"You'd take me off the case?"

"In a heartbeat," said Sam. "No case is worth your life."

Angie sat back in her chair and directed her gaze at her lap. "It wouldn't come to that."

"It might, but it won't," said Adam. "Because you will have a protective detail. And so will Sam."

Sam glanced at him, eyes wide with surprise. "Adam, I don't—"

"I'm glad we had a chance to settle this," said Adam as he turned and walked away.

Sam turned to Angie and cocked an eyebrow.

She grinned at him. "Good for the goose, and all that."

7

Two weeks later, as Sam and Angie climbed the wide stone steps to the courthouse, trailed by their obvious protective details of thick limbed therianthropes, a giant of a wizard came down to meet them. He wore a meticulously tailored black suit under a heavy overcoat.

"Verbius!" said Angie. "What are you doing here?"

Verbius shook his head once, his face grim. "I hate to do this to you, Angie." He nodded at Sam. "Mr. McCoy."

"What's going on?"

"I've...uh... I have to assert jurisdiction in the Van Dee case."

"No!" said Sam. "You can't have it!"

Verbius grimaced. "I'm afraid I have no choice. The order came down from the Magister General this morning."

"Why, Verbius?" asked Angie. "Why now?"

The tall man rubbed his eyes. "I know it's short notice—"

"No notice is more like it!" snapped Sam. "We're on our way to court this very instant!"

"Paul Leibman has offered the Covenancy a deal, and the Magister General wants to take it."

"The mythical super-cabal of zombie mafiosi? Leibman offered us that, but there's no corroboration! Nothing to indicate it could survive even if Rose Marie Van Dee was not about to go to prison for the rest of her life!" Angie looked up at Verbius with a pleading gaze.

"I'm afraid—"

"No!" snapped Sam. "I won't stand for this. We're due in court, Verbius." With that, he turned and started up the steps.

Angie's lips drew into a line as she turned to follow.

"You're wasting your time," said Verbius with a sigh. "Your case has been transferred to Covenancy Court."

She whirled back to face him. "Why? Just tell me that!"

"I already said: the Magister General wants to make a deal. To get to the bigger fish—or at least other bosses as powerful as Van Dee."

"Maybe so, Verbius, but there's a right way and a wrong way to do this. You know that as well as I do, and I want to know why you decided to do it the wrong way."

Verbius averted his gaze and shook his head. "Angie, I'm only doing what I've been told—"

"Save it!" she snapped, then turned and ran up the steps to catch Sam before he went inside.

8

Adam handed Sam a drink in a cut-crystal glass and sat in the armchair next to the couch where Sam slouched. "The Magister General wants this to happen, Sam."

"You have to do something, Adam!"

"What's there to do?" The Locus Magister spread his hands. "They are within their rights to assert jurisdiction under the TICO Act. You know that, Sam."

Sam scoffed. "Theurgist Influenced Cabalistic Organization? They don't have the requisite charges to prosecute anyone under the act but their star witness!"

Adam treated him to a slow nod. "That may be true, Sam, but that's kind of the point. Van Dee is offering to give them enough to take down zombie Cabals from here to Chicago."

"Murder, Adam! We have the evidence to get multiple convictions. They can have her after I'm finished!"

Adam chuckled. "You know it doesn't work that way."

"I'm not dropping the charges! I won't do it. The Locus of New York demands justice!"

"So now *you* speak for the Locus of New York?" asked Adam with exasperation etching lines into his face. "I seem to have missed the election."

"When you asked me—*asked me*—to take this job, Adam, you promised me—*promised me*—that you wouldn't let politics get in my way."

"And I haven't, Sam, not once." Adam sipped his Scotch and set it on the table. "I understand your frustration, but these things happen. The Covenancy wants her, and the Covenancy will have her."

Sam grunted, shook his head once, and looked into his own glass of Scotch before downing it. "I'm not going to let her go without a fight, Adam," he said in a quiet, flat tone.

"What are you going to do? Argue your case in Covenancy Court? Who do you think will win that case?"

"If I don't win, I'll appeal."

"And then what?"

"I'll go all the way to Washington if I have to."

Adam's expression fell into angry lines. "Then you'd better get to it, Sam," he growled, lifting both hands toward him with his palms up and shooed him away.

Sam nodded and left his office.

9

Sam glanced at Verbius as he came through the swinging gates in the bar. He set his briefcase down and pulled out the chair to sit, but then he turned to the Covenancy Magister. "We don't have to do this, you know."

Verbius tilted his head to the side. "Oh, I think you're wrong there."

"Withdraw jurisdiction until after I prosecute her," urged Sam. "It will help your case to have several felony convictions against her."

Verbius shook his head, looking down at the polished tabletop. "No, it won't, and you know it. If anyone levels charges against her, she clams up. You know how this works, McCoy." He looked at Sam askance. "Besides, your foolish motion threatens to undercut the Covenancy's ability to act. Surely you recognized that the Magister General would order a response."

"I never thought I'd have to fight my own government to get a fair shake at prosecuting a zombie crime boss."

Verbius shrugged and gave him a sour smile. "And I never thought I'd have to defend my jurisdiction over the Southern District of the Locus of New York."

Sam frowned and turned away.

"All rise!" cried the bailiff.

Sam turned and watched Judge Rhea Dubativo ascend to the bench, moving with the careful plodding of great age. She walked with two canes, her back bent and humped between her shoulders, her long, stringy hair almost obscuring her face. The hem of the long, black velvet robe she wore dragged on the floor.

She took her seat and shot a rheumy-eyed glare at Sam. "Let's get this foolishness finished." She reached for her gavel with a shaking hand, swept it up, and banged it harshly on the sound block. "I've read the briefs, so let's not waste time rehashing the Executive Assistant Locus Magister for the Locus of New York's spurious claim. Anything new to add to yer ridiculous motion, Mr. McCoy?"

"Your Honor, I must object to—"

"Overruled."

"But I—"

"Are ye deaf, cully? I've overruled yer God-pounding objection!"

Sam snapped his mouth shut. He'd never argued a motion before Rhea Dubativo before, but he'd heard of her eccentricities, her rages. Adam had warned him not to get her riled, and inside of the first few minutes, it seemed he'd managed to do just that. "I apologize to the Court," he said.

"Stop that groveling, Sai McCoy—sniveling catches in my brains like a fishhook, it does!"

"Yes, Your Honor."

"Now then, I asked ye a question, and I'll have an answer from ye." A petulant frown decorated her face as she squinted down at him shrewdly.

"Yes, Your Honor. My brief contains the bulk of my argument."

"It does, does it?" She threw her head back and cackled up at the ceiling. When she finished, she turned her ancient regard on Verbius. "And ye, Mr. Covenancy Magister for the Southern District of the Locus of New

York? Have ye more drivel to add to this refuse I hold before me?"

Sam's brow wrinkled in confusion. It seemed the judge held both arguments in equal contempt. And both magisters, as well.

"Nay, Yer Honor," said Verbius.

McCoy cast a quick glance at him. "Your Honor, if I may be so bold—"

"Bold. Yes, cully. Bold, y'are. Bold, y'are."

"Uh, yes, Your Honor. As I was saying, I'd—"

"Oh, no, cully! Ye'll not wag a pert tongue at me, lest ye find it lying as still as an old dead viper in yer maw."

"I apologize, Your Honor. It seems I'm off to a bad start. Perhaps I can begin anew?"

Dubativo leaned her head back to stare down her nose at him. Her eyelids drooped into a squint, and the only sound in the courtroom came from the ticking clock. "Nay, nay, yon clock beats as steady as a God's ugly heart, and there's no turning it back." The corners of her mouth turned down, but it was a frown of hard thought rather than displeasure. "Yet mayhap we'll go forward better than we've begun. Adam Hill be a powerful enemy to make, and I'd not make that mistake."

Sam had no idea how she expected him to respond to that, so he applied a rule his father had taught him—it's better to look foolish for saying nothing at all than paint himself a fool by saying something stupid.

Old Rhea nodded as though she'd read the thought straight out of his mind and approved of its sentiment. "So, let's have it, then. Speak yer piece, McCoy, and we'll see if ancient Verbius, here, can dance as well as ye have."

"Thank you, Judge Dubativo." Sam looked down for a moment to gather his thoughts in order. When he raised his head, he found Rhea Dubativo's penetrating gaze waiting for him.

"Your Honor, heinous crimes have been committed against the people of the Locus of New York. Horrible crimes that resulted in dismemberment, death, and worse, for mundanes and supernaturals alike. My learned colleague asserts that the Covenancy's claim on justice is the higher, but without these charges filed in the Locus of New York, the Covenancy lacks the requisite felonies to bring TICO charges against Rose Marie Van Dee. If they are allowed to quash these charges, Ms. Van Dee can simply change her mind, and Verbius won't have a leg to stand on."

"Aye, aye. As much you said in yer brief, Mr. McCoy. I was wanting to hear *new* arguments, not the same one already written, trussed up with fine language as it was."

McCoy looked down at the table for a moment, then said, "Your Honor, Ms. Van Dee is the head of the Zombie mafia in the Locus of New York. She's never stood for criminal charges levied against her; she's never even been close to the defendant's table before. Why? It's simple. She is insulated from the day-to-day evils of her organization. She has cut-outs in place, and we've never before had the leverage to get past those cut-outs. The People—"

"And ye do now?"

McCoy nodded. "Yes, we do, Your Honor. We have eye-witness testimony. We can lock Van Dee up for a lifetime at the very least."

"And ye, old Verbius? What have ye to say?"

"Judge, my learned opponent's arguments notwithstanding, the Covenancy has the right to assert—"

"Oh, nay, nay, nay, sirrah. I'll not hear of rights and domains, and suchlike, nay. I'll hear yer argue of real things. People and places, good and bad."

"But, Your Honor," said Verbius. "The Canon and Covenants explicitly address this issue in—"

"Are ye deaf, cully? Did yer betters never teach ye better than to persist in foolishness when warned against it?"

"I'm sorry, Your Honor."

"And well ye should be, Sai Verbius. And well ye should be. Have ye more to say?"

Verbius frowned. "Could I have a moment to collect my thoughts?"

"Hurry, for your father's sake! I've more to do this fine day than listen to the likes of ye."

After clearing his throat, Verbius lifted his head. "Judge Dubativo, you have asked me to couch my arguments in the everyday rather than the tenets of the Covenancy. If Mr. McCoy is allowed to quash our jurisdiction, the Covenancy will be in grave danger. Ms. Van Dee has information that we can use to stamp out the Zombie mafia across several Loci, and if Mr. McCoy proceeds with his reckless charges, she will keep that information in the dark corners of her heart, leaving many others to suffer."

"What care have I for the suffering of others? What care have I for the fate of other Loci?"

"You don't mean that, Your Honor!"

"Do I not?" Old Rhea threw back her head and cackled at the ceiling. "Hee! Ye may speak true, Verbius—and ye may not, mind—but what difference does it make? Why should the suffering of people in a far-off Locus trump the suffering of the people in this Locus?"

"Judge, we must look to the greater good. We must protect our society as a whole."

"Must we?" asked Rhea, in an almost wistful tone.

"We must," said Verbius with a stiff nod.

"Then tell me, sirrah. How do I define this greater good ye speak of?"

"In our society, we all make sacrifices—we all act for the many, rather than for ourselves. We obey the Covenant of Improper Action. For example, vampires obtain licenses to drink from the necks of the willing. And to do otherwise, Your Honor, would lead to chaos— the mundanes we rule would rise up against us, werewolves would go to war against vampires, demons against angels—these are but examples of the chaos that would ensue should the Covenancy fall."

"Oh, aye," said Rhea with a twinkle in her eye. "And witches would live in old shacks beyond the edges of town, ignored save when some pert girl needs her honesty proved, save when someone needs a bit o' darkness hurled at his fellows."

"Just so, Your Honor," said Verbius.

"Claptrap."

Verbius jerked his head back, a grimace of fury darkening his features. "I beg your pardon, Your Honor?"

"Yea, 'tis nothing but bunk ye've rolled out on yer tongue like a peppermint. 'Tis nothing more likely to occur than the Sun turning to gold and dropping into my pocket. 'Tis the fiction of a great mind, no doubt, but in this world, cully, in this world, *we* run the show. Those beneath our feet could no more rise up than ye could sprout flapping wings to ride the winds to far and away. Nay, cully. Yer argument doesn't persuade."

Verbius could do no more than stand and stare, while Sam felt the beginnings of a grin on his lips.

Rhea Dubativo turned her hawk-like gaze on Sam, and her eyes narrowed. "Oh, don't get smug, Sai McCoy. 'Twas only of marginal improvement, yer argument." She leaned back and released a heavy sigh. "Would that I could send ye both away, shunned and chastened... But alas, I cannot." She reached for the gavel and drew it to her chest. "In this matter, The

People of the Locus of New York versus the Covenancy, I, Rhea Dubativo, Weirdling of the Cöos, hereby quash the Covenancy's assertion of jurisdiction in the matter of the People versus Rose Marie Van Dee." She glared at McCoy for a moment before turning her baleful gaze on Verbius. "Ye can have her when Sai McCoy finishes with her." She rapped the gavel on the sound block, then turned and made her ponderous way to her chambers.

Smiling, McCoy packed away his things and turned to go. Verbius stood at his table, looking stricken and surprised. "Don't take it so hard, Verbius."

"It makes no sense, Sam. Surely, you must see that the Covenancy has to be free to make deals to—"

"Like the old crone said, you can have her when I'm finished. Guilty verdicts can only help you, Verbius."

Shaking his head, Verbius turned and left the courtroom without another word.

10

Adam Hill swept the door open with a crash and stood in the hall glowering at Sam. "You're happy, now? I certainly hope so. You've managed to alienate the Magister General and half the Covenancy with your little ploy."

Sam pushed away from his desk and swiveled in his chair to face the door. "I couldn't let her get away with everything she's done, Adam."

"Of course, you couldn't! Sam The Stakeman McCoy never loses a case!"

"It's not about me—"

"*Of course it is*! You'd better make good on this mess, Sam!" Adam whirled and stomped away, just as Angie entered Sam's office from the other door.

"Uh oh," she said. "Is Daddy mad?"

Sam treated her to a smile. "He is, but he'll get over it when we convict Van Dee."

"I heard he's been on the phone to the Magister General himself for the past hour."

"I thought his ass looked a little chewed."

"And how's yours looking?"

"Don't worry about me. If Adam was really angry, he'd have my resignation already."

Angie looked at the empty doorway for a moment before crossing the office to close the door. "We might have a little trouble from Jack Barnett."

"I doubt it. It's far too late for him to go back to Rose Marie."

"He's grumpy about his limbs. Or rather, the lack of them."

Sam chuckled and shook his head once. "He can't possibly expect the Locus of New York to replace limbs he lost trying to kill a police officer."

Angie shrugged with her eyebrows and hitched one side of her mouth up. "It seems he can."

McCoy lifted his eyebrows and scoffed. "The nerve of that guy."

"He's only half the problem."

"His girlfriend."

"Guessed it in one. She says if Jack isn't happy, she isn't happy."

"Isn't she the one who was so worried about having her parts spread all across the countryside?"

"Yes, but they seem to have recognized we're sunk without them."

"But we have no control over the Body Part Procurement and Transport Network! We can put him on the list, but it'll take years to work his way to the top."

Angie nodded. "The Van Dee Cabal is in the body parts business because of the BPPTN's legendary slowness. He says Mama Zombie can get him the parts he needs tomorrow. No list, no muss, no fuss."

"How does he know that? Have they contacted their former associates?"

"Leery says they haven't." Angie shrugged and flopped herself into an empty chair. "Barnett claims he could make a call and have fresh parts within a few hours, then one of their pet morticians would come and connect them up."

"And what about repercussions for squealing?"

Angie heaved a sigh. "He claims that after they'd been left to rot for a few decades, Rose Marie would gather them back up and put them to work. He also says they would have no memories of the time. It's like being in a coma, evidently."

"He's bluffing!"

Angie pulled on her bottom lip. "Maybe so."

"Even if he isn't, there's nothing we can do. The BPPTN is an independent organization for a reason."

"Yeah."

"You don't seem sure."

"No, it's..." Angie pulled on her lip, staring past Sam and out the window.

"It's what?"

Moving with slow deliberation, she turned her gaze to meet his. "The thing is, we *can* get him replacement parts."

"What? How?"

"We already have them—in the SIS evidence locker. And both Jack and Dee know we have them."

Sam lifted his chin, his face devoid of emotion. "From the raid."

Angie nodded.

"You can't be serious!"

"Look, Sam, I'm trying to solve this problem. This is the only way I see us getting past it, short of calling Rose Marie's newest chop shop and putting in an order."

"Here's an idea. What if we drop Jack Barnett into general population under Rikers? *Without* new limbs."

"He'd be chopped up and spread around the dungeon within a day."

Sam shrugged. "Probably, but you don't know that for sure."

"And what? Let Rose Marie Van Dee go?"

"This Dee Terry would come around after she sees what befalls her friend."

"That's a bad idea, Sam. Really bad."

"Stealing and illegally distributing evidence is a better idea?"

Angie returned his gaze with calm detachment. "We don't need to steal it. We have plenty of parts from the raid. Who's to say we don't release certain items for disposal?"

Sam sucked his teeth and shook his head once. "There's no other way?"

"Not that I can see."

"Set it up, then," he said with a sigh.

II

Jack wobbled out of the room behind Dee and Dru, still a little unsteady on his feet. "I swear one of these legs is the wrong length."

"Nah, I measured 'em. They are exact matches."

Dee scoffed. "One is Asian, and one is white, Oriscoe."

"Ah, but they're the same length." He took a swig of coffee. "Come on. We don't want to be late for the big show. And make sure you got everything. We won't be coming back here."

"Thank goodness for that." Dee glanced around, looking like a ferret checking for predators. "I can't believe there's only two of you."

"Relax," said Dru. "No one knows where this dump is."

They climbed down the stairs to the underground parking lot and pushed out into the damp, dark space. "The car's pretty close," said Leery, tossing his empty coffee cup on the ground. "Follow me." He took off, but neither Dee nor Jack moved an inch, and he stopped and turned back. "What is it now?"

Dee pointed at two white vans parked at the other end of the row.

"Work vans. So what?"

"We know those vans," said Jack. "Our...uh...retrieval teams drive vans like that."

"Yeah, your retrieval teams and every workman in the city. Come on." He turned and continued walking to his dark blue Crown

Victoria. He popped the trunk when he arrived and shuffled things around, trying to make room for Dee and Jack's bags.

Dru approached, shaking her head. "You couldn't have cleaned this out before?"

"What, and miss the fun of you telling me I should've done it before? Nah." He pulled a brass *menorah* and his black woolen hat from the trunk. "Hold these, will you?"

"A *menorah*? Why are you carting this around? It's nowhere near Hanukkah. You need to get that beast inside you under control."

"Yeah, because werewolves aren't stubborn at all." He waved at Dee and Jack, who had lagged behind. "Come on, slowpokes."

Jack glared at him and opened his mouth to speak, but his gaze shifted to something behind Leery, and he loosed an incoherent cry instead.

Leery whirled to see the back doors of both white vans disgorging zombies. "Great," he muttered and began a rapid transformation, tearing his clothes asunder. Dru dropped the *menorah* and the hat and traced fourteen small runes in the air, then connected them with a chartreuse seven-pointed star. Leery stooped and scooped up the hat and the *menorah,* seating the first on his lupine skull and grasping the second by its base. As Dru connected the last point of the star, a brilliant red-orange light flared around the rune set, stabbing into even the darkest corners of the garage.

For a moment, the attacking zombies froze in that coquelicot-colored light, but only for a moment. With harsh cries, they sprinted toward the Crown Victoria.

Leery snarled at the oncoming zombies and swung the *menorah* at the first of them, braining him and sending enough gore flying to please any splatterpunk fan. The zombie he struck spun in a half-circle, his jaw flapping soundlessly as he pitched to the concrete.

"Down!" Dru shouted, and Leery dropped to the ground. She barked a harsh word in the *Verba Patiendi,* and the blood garnet on the end of her staff blazed with blood-red light. Her rune set pulsed, once, twice, and then began to spin counterclockwise. Brilliant orange and vermillion flames exploded outward from the seven-pointed star, hissing through the air like God's own vengeance.

Zombies caught in the blast sizzled and popped like dry, sap-filled wood, then burst into flame, gushing greasy black smoke. But they came on anyway, a tide of burning putrescence.

Leery shot a look at Dru over his shoulder and barked, jerking his chin toward the car. Without waiting to see that she did as he wanted—or even that she understood—he sprang toward the wave of charging zombies, holding the *menorah* high above his head like a cudgel.

Dru turned to their charges and yelled, "Get in the damn car!" Then ran for the driver's side door.

Leery landed square in the middle of the zombie horde and swung the *menorah* like an avenging angel. His *payot* flew as he spun side to side, laying about himself with both *menorah* and claw. Behind him, Dru barked a word of power, that rang in his ears, followed by the familiar tingle of a ward settling on his shoulders.

The zombies circled him, keeping wary eyes on the whistling *menorah* and wicked claws. He spun in circles, slashing, bashing, kicking, snapping his teeth, but there were too many of them—at least twenty once-human candles circled him, sizzling fat and melting skin dripping to the concrete.

When he heard the Crown Vic's eight-cylinder engine roar to life, Leery howled. Tires screeching, the car whipped by, smashing through the zombies on his left and hurling them through the air. With a snarl, Leery jabbed the *menorah* at the remaining zombies, then sprinted after the car, pouring on every ounce of speed his wolf form had to spare.

The zombies chased him up the ramp that led to the street, screaming with rage. Leery caught the tail of the Crown Vic sliding around the corner down the block, and his lips peeled back in the wolf equivalent of a smile. He pelted for the alley across the street. His hat tried to come off in the wind generated by his passage, but he slapped a hand on top of his head, still grasping the *menorah* in the other.

The alley was cool and dark in the watery gray light of early morning, and he blended in as if made for urban stealth, flickering from shadow to shadow. A few of the fastest zombies reached the mouth of the alley behind him, raising a cry and starting after him.

Dru brought the car to a screeching halt at the other end of the alley and flung the passenger door open. Leery put his head down and poured on the speed.

He bounded into the car, changing his skin in midair, and Dru floored it, racing away from the alley before he'd even closed the door.

"I called it in on the way around the block," said Dru. "Van Helsing is sending in SWAT—ones she knows aren't bent."

"Good. It would serve those dead bastards right to get stomped on a little bit." Leery blew out a long breath, looking at a long burn that stretched the length of his right forearm. He glanced at the two zombies in the back seat. "That's two sets of clothes you two owe me," he groused.

"Are you alright?" asked Dru, darting a glance at him.

"Let's see... Naked, a little bit singed, carrying a *menorah* and a black hat. Yep. I'm fine." He shifted the hat from his head to cover his lap. "Can't go to court like this, though."

A smile quirked the side of Dru's mouth he could see. "I could slap an illusion on you."

"That wouldn't help with the draft. Head back to the Two-seven. It's on the way." He turned a sunny smile her way. "And I can get another cup of coffee there."

Dru shook her head but couldn't keep the grin off her face.

12

cCoy glanced back as Leery stuck his head in through the hall door. Sam arched his eyebrows, and Leery nodded. "They're here," he said to Angie.

"Thank the Power," she breathed. "It's about time."

"All rise!" shouted the extremely short bailiff with a long flowing beard. He banged the butt of his archaic and brutal-looking halberd on the floor. "Order, order! I call this court to order, the Just and Honorable Grimhildr Gyuki presiding."

As everyone got to their feet, a beautiful red-haired woman appeared on the bench in a flash of sharp blue light and a cloud of white smoke. She smiled at the bailiff. "Thank you, Thoridn."

The short man ducked his chin in a respectful salute and snapped his heels together.

The redhead turned her gaze on the prosecution table and gave McCoy a wink and a single nod. "Mr. McCoy."

"Judge Gyuki," he replied. "It's nice to see you again."

"Likewise." She turned her attention on the defense table. "And Mr. Leibman, is it?"

"Yes, Your Honor."

"I haven't had the pleasure of your presence in my courtroom before, have I?"

"Only once, Your Honor, and it was many years ago."

An expression of consternation wrinkled Judge Gyuki's brow, a cloud passing before the sun on a warm spring day. "Is it so?" She picked up her gavel, but her eyes never left Paul Leibman's. "I don't recall, and for that, I apologize."

"It's nothing to concern yourself over, Your Honor. It was a trivial case, disposed of in short order."

"Aha. Perhaps that explains it." She lifted the gavel and snapped it down on the sound block. "And do you represent all the defendants in today's trial?"

"Yes, Your Honor. I have the honor of representing Rose Marie Van Dee, Lothidn Oorskowkinum, and *Shuten-doji*."

Gyuki treated the defense table with a single, brisk nod. "Since all parties are present, I see no reason for further delay.

Court is now in session." Her gaze danced between McCoy and Leibman. "Gentlemen, I expect a clean fight. No...drat, what's the word..." She turned toward Thoridn. "*Tvowfeldni*?"

"Duplicity, Your Grace."

"Aha. Yes. No duplicity from either quarter. No chicanery. I'll not have it. Do you both understand?"

Both McCoy and Leibman said they did.

"Very well. Mr. McCoy, begin."

"Thank you, Your Honor." Sam stood and walked around the table to face the jury. He looked each one in the eye, then dropped his chin and put his hands behind his back. "Ladies and gentlemen of the jury, during the course of this trial, you may find your ethics—and, indeed, your morals—tested. The woman seated at the defense table behind me is Rose Marie Van Dee, and she stands accused of crimes both various and sundry, but there is no charge in our beloved Canon and Covenants that covers her ultimate crime. Many of you know that this Locus has a problem with occult cabals.

"You've no doubt heard of the Zombie mafia. Perhaps you've seen romanticized movies or television programs dealing with the subject.

You may have read fictional accounts that paint mafia life as honorable—misunderstood underdogs fighting against a corrupt system. Let me assure you, here and now, that there is nothing honorable or romantic about the Zombie mafia. They are nothing but thugs, extorting what they want through fear and brutality." He spun on his heel and pointed at Van Dee. "The woman you see here, ladies and gentlemen, is Rose Marie Van Dee, the so-called Mama Zombie of the Locus of New York, and head of the Van Dee Cabal."

Rose Marie trotted out her best grandmother smile and winked at the jury.

"Despite what she'd like you to believe," said McCoy, "she's not a sweet old lady trapped in undeath by powers out of her control. No, we will present evidence to the contrary... Evidence that proves Rose Marie Van Dee is a tyrant who rules the occult cabal in this Locus with an iron fist, with the threat of torture and worse. She is responsible for a string of murders of the mundanes we share this Locus with, for the purpose of harvesting their body parts." Several members of the jury gasped, and McCoy nodded. "Yes, that's correct. In order to generate inventory for her chop shops, the defendant hired mercenaries to kill unsuspecting mundanes without a permit, out of season, and outside the auspices of the Covenant of Improper Action. You will hear from some of these mercenaries as they give direct testimony of their own crimes in order to implicate Ms. Van Dee."

McCoy turned and paced back and forth in front of the jury box. "That Rose Marie Van Dee gave the orders in this venture cannot be disputed, yet we will provide evidence in the form of eye-witness zombie testimony to those orders. But"—McCoy held up his index finger like a schoolmarm lecturing her class—"her crimes and, yea, her charges, do not end with that. The People also levy multiple charges of bribery in the first degree, intimidation of a law enforcement official, obstruction of justice, and perverting the course of justice." McCoy turned his back on the defense table and showed his best smile to the jury, eyes crinkling with benevolence. "And this brings us back to the very first thing I said to you, ladies and gentlemen—that this case may test your ethics and morality.

"'How so?' you might ask. Well, the answer is simple: you may be approached by Ms. Van Dee's underlings and either wooed or threatened to influence your decision in this case." McCoy paused and lifted his shoulders. "It has happened before, and it *will* happen again. But I find it necessary to advise you from the perspective of Covenancy law. If you are wooed—and this may take the form of bribery with cash, either direct or indirect, or *any other thing of value*—then you are committing a felony. We will discover it, and you will find yourself seated where Ms. Van Dee and her co-defendants now sit. And let me tell you, those seats are *most* uncomfortable. But you know all this." Sam flashed his kind smile again. "What you may not know, and what Ms. Van Dee's minions will take great pains to conceal from you, is that if you succumb to their threats, their enticements, they will see you as a *liability*." McCoy paused and met each of their gazes. "And how do you think the Zombie mafia deals with liabilities?" He turned and looked at the defense. "Well, I think we all know how that is accomplished."

"Your Honor, I must object to this," said Leibman. "Mr. McCoy is casting—"

"It's his opening statement, sir, and you will have your turn. Overruled."

"Thank you, Judge Gyuki," said McCoy. He faced the jury once more, but before he could begin again, Lieutenant Van Helsing drifted into the court and approached the bar. Angie leaned toward her, and Epatha whispered in her ear. Carmichael's eyes widened, and she beckoned Sam.

"I beg your pardon, Your Honor," said McCoy as he approached the prosecution table. He bent over it and listened, then glanced at Van Helsing. When she nodded, Sam turned to face the Court, his face set in grim lines. "Your Honor, please allow this to serve as the People's notice that we will be amending the charges against Rose Marie Van Dee to include two counts of witness tampering, two counts of assault on a law enforcement officer, one count of battery on a law enforcement officer, and one count of attempted murder of a law enforcement officer. Let me add that we will be extending the scope of our examination of witnesses Leery Oriscoe, Drusilla Nogan, Dee Terry, and Jack Barnett."

"It is within your purview to do so, Mr. McCoy. Clerk, please note the additions. Continue, Mr. McCoy."

"Thank you, Your Honor." He faced Rose Marie Van Dee. "In the interest of justice, Your Honor, I'd like the defendant held in complete isolation for the remainder of the trial."

"Your Honor, I must—"

"I understand that order is already in place, Mr. McCoy. Sit down, Mr. Leibman."

"Thank you, Judge Gyuki. I only wish to request that the isolation order not be lifted." Sam turned and faced the jury once more. "You've just witnessed another of the ways the defendant will try to manipulate this trial: violence against my witnesses. Don't let her succeed. In this case, you will hear ugly truths like this one, but *truths*. The defense will try to skew those truths. They will try to cast them in a suspicious or scornful light. Do not be deceived. Thank you for your attention." Sam turned and took his seat.

"Very well, Mr. McCoy," said Judge Gyuki. She waved a languid hand at Paul Leibman.

"Thank you, Your Honor," he said, gaining his feet. "Ladies and gentlemen of the jury, my opponent, Mr. McCoy, spoke of many things, but he left some salient points unsaid. First, he may present what he calls eyewitnesses. I call them conspirators, and even Mr. McCoy must admit to the truth of *that* statement. These people are testifying only to avoid prosecution for *murder* and more. They have concocted this insane story implicating my clients with one—and *only* one—motive in mind: to save their own skins. Ask yourselves if the statement of a co-conspirator in the alleged crime is enough 'proof' to justify a verdict of guilty beyond a reasonable doubt. Assess the character of these witnesses, examine their past behavior, and contrast both to that of my clients—two respectable small business owners and a poor troll working to better his environment. I promise you: you will find these eyewitnesses lacking." Leibman turned and faced Sam. "And I'd like you to consider another point and another man's character. The prosecutor-in-chief, Sam McCoy, has gone to great lengths to seat Ms. Van Dee before you. He won't want to share those lengths with you. Suffice it to say he brought an action against the very Covenancy we all hold dear."

McCoy chuckled and shook his head.

"This man has an agenda. This man has something against my clients. This man is the one presenting you with skewed truths. This—"

"Mr. Leibman?" asked Grimhildr Gyuki. "You allege what amounts to serious charges against an officer of the court in good standing. Are you sure you wish to proceed in this vein? I will hold you accountable."

"I apologize to the Court and to Mr. McCoy. I intended only to illustrate the flaws of his argument, not to accuse him of criminal acts."

"Proceed, then, Mr. Leibman, but I'll have no more of that, if you please."

"Yes, Judge." Leibman turned back to the jury and offered a weak smile. "In the interest of truth, I do not mean to impugn Mr. McCoy in any way except for misguided zeal and passion for his profession. In fact, Mr. McCoy and I have known one another for decades." He turned and smiled at Sam. "I count him as a friend, and though I may have gotten carried away a moment ago, I assure you of his good character and intentions." Turning back to the jury, he smiled, this time with a predatory gleam in his eye. "But as his friend of so many years, I am well suited to point out his errors, his flaws. In this case, one of the qualities that makes him such a good Locus Magister has led him down the garden path, so to speak. As long as I have known him, tenaciousness has defined him in everything he's pursued—at least in part. He is like the proverbial bulldog, locking his jaws around his prey. In this case, that prey sits at the defense table, weary, worried, and broken-hearted. Do not hold this against, Mr. McCoy"—Leibman darted a glance at Judge Gyuki—"he is only doing what he thinks just. But, please, ladies and gentlemen, do not simply take his word for it. Examine each bit of proof, listen to my cross-examination of each witness, listen to their answers, their *evasions*. At the end of the trial, tally up your scores. Mark those you believed, and those who left you with doubt. Compare the two, and I'm sure you will return a verdict of not guilty on all counts. Thank you." Leibman gave the jury a little bow then returned to his seat.

"Mr. McCoy, present your case."

"Yes, Your Honor. The People call Dee Terry to the stand."

As Dru led her in, Thoridn narrowed his eyes at the zombie and seemed to bristle. He went as far as to growl something under his breath and sneered as she passed. To McCoy, it sounded like "trucker," but knowing Thoridn and Grimhildr's Nordic background, he assumed it was "*truykr*" the Old Norse word for zombie. Thoridn swore Dee in, taking care that they never touched by accident.

McCoy rose and approached the witness box. "Ms. Terry, good morning, and thank you for being here."

"Good morning."

"Before we get into your testimony, first may I inquire about your well-being? I understand you were attacked this morning by a zombie horde."

Dee darted a scathing glance at Rose Marie, who refused to meet her gaze. "Yes, though I wasn't personally attacked, I'm sure that my friend, Jack Barnett, and I were their primary targets."

"Then you aren't injured?"

"No."

"Thank goodness. But if we could return to your statement that you weren't personally attacked—I assume this means someone was?"

"Yes. The zombies came at us, but Detectives Leery Oriscoe and Dru Nogan stood in our defense."

"And one of the detectives was the one you meant?"

"Yes. First, Nogan lit them all aflame, and then Oriscoe waded into their midst in wolf form, distracting and delaying them so we could escape with Nogan."

"I see. Now, you mentioned a zombie horde. I take it you do not mean the kind of mindless zombie hordes seen in video games, movies, and television?"

"No, not at all. Those shows are insulting."

"Then, may I ask, what do you mean when you say, 'zombie horde?'"

"It's what the Zombie mafia calls a group of enforcers sent out to do wet work."

"Wet work?"

"Sure. Kill someone. Beat someone up. Draw blood."

"I understand. And how do you know that the Zombie mafia calls these hit squads by the term 'zombie horde?'"

Dee flashed a lopsided smile at the jury. "Because, until recently, I was a member of the Zombie mafia."

"And were you asked to participate in these hordes?"

"From time to time," said Dee with a shrug. "We all are."

"What message do you draw from this morning's attack?"

Dee's expression darkened. "That Rose Marie doesn't want us to testify."

"That seems reasonable. Tell me, Ms. Terry, did you recognize any of the zombies attacking you?"

"Sure."

"And you will testify against them at their trials?"

Dee barked a harsh laugh that echoed throughout the chamber. "Sure, why not?"

"Why not, indeed. What do you expect their defense will be?"

"Your Honor?" said Leibman, getting to his feet and raising his hand.

"Yes, Mr. Leibman?"

"I fail to see how any of this is relevant to the case at hand. Does Mr. McCoy intend to demonstrate a link to my client?"

Grimhildr arched an eyebrow at Sam.

"Yes, I do, Your Honor. Subsequent to further testimony."

"Then, I'll allow it." Leibman opened his mouth to protest, but Grimhildr shot him a look that could break glass. "Your continued objection is noted and tabled until Mr. McCoy succeeds or fails in demonstrating this link."

Leibman nodded. "Thank you, Your Honor. And the testimony will be stricken if he fails?"

Judge Gyuki nodded, and Leibman regained his seat.

"Ms. Terry? What do you expect the members of the attacking horde to present as their defense at trial?"

"They will claim it was a misunderstanding. That the officers attacked them when they were just playing a prank, and that from there, they were only defending themselves from unjust injury."

"I see. How do you know this?"

Dee chuckled. "That's what Mama Rose Marie told us all to do."

"I see. And to say it explicitly, do you believe Rose Marie Van Dee is behind the attack this morning?"

"Of course."

"Fine. Let's leave the events of this morning for now and turn our attention to the day of your arrest."

"Okay."

"In what activity were you engaged that afternoon?"

"Me and Jack were minding one of the shops."

"Please tell us what is sold in these shops you mention."

"Illegal body parts. Arms, mostly."

"Chop shops?" He waited for her nod, then continued, "And who is your primary clientele?"

"Zombies, of course, though we do get the occasional golem with delusions of grandeur."

Sam tucked his chin against his chest. "Where did your inventory come from?"

"At first, we robbed fresh graves, but demand was heavy, and the butcher, John May, told us a new supplier would bring the parts."

"John May? Is he also a zombie?"

"No. He's one of Rose Marie's playthings."

"Who brought you the new inventory?"

"Sometimes it was a troll, sometimes a bugge."

"An unseelie and a troll? Strange bedfellows."

"They didn't like each other much; I can tell you that."

"Do you know their names?"

"The troll was Lothidn, the big brute at the defense table, and the bugge went by Carden, though I got the feeling that was an alias."

Sam scratched an eyebrow. "And could you identify him?"

"Sure. I already have, for the police."

"Yes, and your identification led to his arrest." He turned to the jury. "We'll hear from him later in the trial." Sam turned and walked back to the prosecution table, taking a sip of water from the glass there. "Tell me, Ms. Terry, do you know where those body parts brought by Lothidn and Carden came from?"

"Not specifically, but they were very fresh. Still warm in most cases."

"Not like the ones stolen from graves, then?"

"No, not at all. Some still bled. They made quite a mess."

"I'm sure they did. Do you know who owned these chop shops?"

Dee lifted her arm and pointed at Rose Marie.

"For the record, please, Ms. Terry," said Grimhildr.

"Rose Marie Van Dee."

"I see," said Sam, turning to look at the jury. "How did you come to know that?"

"She was the one who sent Jack and me to the apartment. Besides, she runs everything in the New York Locus."

"She runs everything?" asked McCoy.

Leibman shot to his feet. "Your Honor!"

"Mr. McCoy, clean it up."

"Yes, Your Honor." He turned to Dee. "Speaking only of things you have direct knowledge of, please tell us the business Rose Marie Van Dee controls."

"Easy," said Dee. "Zombie prostitution, gambling, the protection racket, the chop shops, trade in illegal artifacts, murders for hire. She even brokers mercenary contracts to private warlords in other Loci—both in and outside the Covenancy."

"And I want to stress for the jury that you have *direct* knowledge of these businesses?"

"Yes. Before I convinced her to use me as a soldier, Rose Marie made me keep her books." She turned a withering glare on Van Dee. "I kept *copies.*"

"Your Honor, I present the items V1 through V13 for inclusion into evidence."

"So noted."

Rose Marie leaned in close to Leibman, grabbed his arm, and hissed into his ear—a stream of angry susurration and sibilants.

Gyuki leaned forward and peered at them. "Is there a problem, Mr. Leibman?"

"Uh, no, Your Honor. Nothing at this time."

With a smile, Sam led Dee Terry through the accounting journals of the Van Dee Family, while Rose Marie simmered and shot her murderous glares.

When McCoy yielded, Leibman approached the witness stand, smiling, and said, "Ms. Terry, I have only a few questions for you."

"Whatever."

"Let's start with this morning's so-called attack, shall we? You testified you believe my client is behind the attack. Do you have evidence of her involvement?"

"Evidence? Like what?"

Leibman spread his hands. "Why, I have no idea. Something that physically links my client to those zombies."

"Oh. Does me recognizing them not count?" She darted a glance at Angie.

"Isn't it possible you are mistaken?"

Dee pursed her lips. "I see what you're trying to do, but I've known some of those zees for years."

"Zees?"

"Yeah. Zees. Zombies."

"Oh, I see. How did you know them?"

"I'd see them at Cabal gatherings, or sometimes in the shop after something went wrong and they needed a new limb or two."

"Ah. And is it your testimony that Rose Marie Van Dee accompanied these, uh, zees during those instances?"

"Of course not."

"Isn't it true that you've *never* seen my client with any of those zombies?"

"Well..."

"I'll take that as a no. Does it then stand to reason that your assertion Ms. Van Dee is behind the attack is mere speculation?"

Terry scoffed and rolled her eyes at the jury. "I'm not sure what planet you're from, but let me assure you Mama Rose Marie controls the Zombie mafia in this Locus. *Everyone* knows that."

"Let's talk about this Zombie mafia you keep mentioning." He turned and paced toward McCoy, then spun back, pointing his finger at Dee. "Do you have any evidence that this Zombie mafia even exists?"

"Er..."

"Or that my client was a part of it?"

"I—"

"Or that *you* are a part of it?"

Dee drew herself up and opened her mouth.

"Isn't it true you made the whole thing up to get out of trouble? Didn't you name my client only because the police gave you her name?"

"Your Honor!" McCoy leaped to his feet. "He's badgering the witness. If he's going to ask a question, she should have a chance to answer it."

"I'm afraid I agree with the prosecutor, Mr. Leibman. Objection sustained. Clerk, strike the last five questions from defense counsel. The jury will disregard the exchange."

"Thank you, Your Honor," said Sam, sinking into his seat.

Leibman dropped his chin to his chest, and when he lifted his face, he was smiling. "Thank you, Your Honor. If I may rephrase?"

"Go ahead."

"I believe we can get to the bottom of this with a single question. Ms. Terry, do you personally have a single shred of evidence that the Zombie mafia exists? A paycheck stub? A tax form? Business cards? Anything?"

Dee rolled her eyes. "It's a *secret* occult cabal, sir."

"Ah, yes. The infamous *secret organization.* Don't you think it's convenient that you don't have to prove this organization even exists to land a sweetheart deal from the Locus Magister's office?" He waved his hand. "Never mind. The answer is self-evident."

Shaking her head, Dee shrugged her shoulders.

"Who helped you fabricate the business records previously entered into evidence? Was it someone in Mr. McCoy's office? Ms. Carmichael, perhaps?"

Angie chuckled and rolled her eyes for the jury, and Van Dee hissed at her like a cat in heat.

"I didn't fabricate those records. I fabricated the ones she shows the police and tax man."

"Ah, so you admit to fabricating records?"

"Sure, I cooked her books. That's what she wanted."

Leibman smiled and nodded, then gave a meaningful look to the members of the jury. "And do you have a written record of my client's instructions to do so?"

Dee scoffed. "That's not how this works, Leibman. You, above all, should know that."

Paul's face drained of color. He snapped around and strode to his seat. "No more questions."

Sam looked at him in open suspicion, then turned his gaze on Dee Terry, but she was staring daggers at Rose Marie Van Dee.

"Mr. McCoy?" asked Grimhildr. "Would you care to redirect?"

"Not at this time, Your Honor, but I'd like to reserve the right to recall this witness pending developments."

"Very well." The judge looked at the clock on the wall and took up her gavel. "Let's adjourn for lunch."

13

The rest of the day passed without surprises. Sam elicited the same information from Jack Barnett as he had from Dee Terry, and Leibman made the same allegations and implications. Everyone, including Judge Gyuki, seemed bored with the whole thing, and Sam couldn't blame them. Grimhildr adjourned the court, stifling a yawn.

"It's time to pass Terry and Barnett off to the Covenancy Marshals," Angie said. "Unless you want Dee in the witness room for easy recall?"

Sam shook his head. "No, send them on. I may recall her, but I hope I don't have to. Let the Covenancy babysit them until I know."

"Right. In that case, I'm off with Oriscoe and Nogan to do the handoff." She treated him to a crooked smile. "Don't look so glum, Sam. Leibman can posture all he wants, but everyone knows the Zombie mafia is real."

"It's not that," Sam said with a frown.

"What, then?"

"'That's not how it works, Leibman. You, above all, should know that.' That's what Terry said."

"Yes, and then Leibman almost ran back to the defense table."

"Like a dog with his tail between his legs."

Angie cocked her head to the side, her long, sable hair cascading off her shoulder. "You don't think..."

"I hope not."

"Should I look into it?"

Sam shook his head, his eyes far away. "Let me talk to him first."

"I don't think that's a good idea, Sam."

"It probably isn't, but I'm going to do it anyway."

"Well, I hope you know what you're doing."

"Me, too, Angie. Me, too."

14

Leery led Dru, Dee, Jack, and Angie down the stairs to the Pearl Street side entrance. He'd set the meeting with the Marshal Service for five, right after court let out, and he already had the zombies' gear in hand. "Well, I haven't hated spending so much time with you two," he said as he pushed out into the cold afternoon air.

"Likewise, smartass," said Jack.

"One of you Oriscoe?" asked a tall ebony-skinned man in a dark suit.

"God, I hope not," said Leery. "I hear that guy's a nutcase."

Shaking her head, Dru hooked her thumb at him. "That's him. I'm Dru Nogan, and this is our Assistant Locus Magister, Angie Carmichael."

"Then these two must be our charges?" he asked, his face grim and cold.

"Dee Terry and Jack Barnett," said Jack.

The black man shook his head. "No longer. Once we're underway, my partner will brief you on your temporary identities."

A short fireplug of a man stepped toward the rear of their car and opened the door. "We're right here," he said in a voice that sounded like a big rig grinding into first gear. "Hope you have everything. You won't be coming back."

"Yeah, about that," said Leery. "Terry may be recalled, but we'll give you plenty of notice."

The squat man turned a dead-eyed stare on Oriscoe. "Do that."

"Well, it's been nice knowing you, Dee. Again."

"Right. Get stuffed, Oriscoe."

"That's the innocent girl I remember."

Dee and Jack slid into the back of the black Lincoln, and the short man walked around to the other side and opened his door.

"Say, we never did get your names," said Leery.

"No, you didn't," said the tall black man. He turned and climbed into the driver's seat. When his partner got in, he cranked up the engine and backed away.

"Nice fella, that guy," said Leery.

"Must have been a postman before joining the Marshals," said Angie. "Bet he hates dogs."

"Very funny," said Leery. "So, where are you parked, counselor?"

"I'm not. I shared a cab with Sam, but he's got something to do."

Leery looked up and down the sidewalk. "Planning on walking back?"

"On a nice day like this? Walking nine miles in these heels would be hell, anyway." She flapped a hand at the gray, overcast sky. "I wouldn't say no to a ride in a cop car."

"We're this way," said Leery gesturing away from Centre street.

"Play your cards right, and I'll buy you a cup of joe, Leery."

"Now we're talking."

15

They came out of the Starbucks down the block from the building that the LM's office shared with the Manhattan District Attorney, Angie holding a short coffee with the familiar green logo on the side in each hand. She passed one of the small cups to Dru and grinned at Leery, who held a *trenta* in each hand. Angie gestured at him with her cup. "Where do you put it all?"

"Everywhere I go, the same question. A guy's gotta have some secrets, right?"

Angie grinned and glanced at Dru. "Seven sugars? I guess you never developed the taste for it?"

"I like it sweet." Dru sniffed and looked away.

"Well, I better get back," said Angie. "Thanks for the lift."

"Anytime, Carmichael," said Leery. He turned the other way, toward where he'd double-parked their car. "Come on, Dru. Don't get all mushy." He started up the block, taking a gulp from each cup.

"Something's bothering me, Leery."

"Yeah? What's that, Dru?"

"Those Marshals."

"Spit it out, Nogan. I'm not a mind-reader, you know."

"Something felt..." She shook her head. "They didn't act right."

"Eh. Those Covenancy pricks sometimes get a stick up their—"

"No, it's more than that. More than ego. They never gave us their names."

"Nope."

"And that car..."

"What? It was a little flashy, I'll grant you, but they *are* Covenancy pricks."

"I don't think Lincolns are used by any service, Leery. It's too expensive for—" A scream from behind them interrupted her, and they both spun around.

Halfway down the block on 125th Street, Angie darted out into the street, accompanied by the screech of tires. Her hat was gone, and one of her sleeves was torn at the shoulder.

"Angie," Dru murmured. Fingers dancing in the air, she started up the street at a run.

Leery tossed his coffees away and burst from his clothes with a sigh that turned into a snarl as he let his darker half out to play. He howled and charged down the middle of the sidewalk, ignoring the mundanes who shrank away in terror.

Dru glanced his way and quickly sketched an illusion with her free hand, uttered a sharp word, and threw it at him. Angie stopped on the double yellow lines and turned to face the way she'd come. Then, she, too, began a spell. Leery poured on the speed, ignoring the traffic, pelting between cars where he could, and over them when he couldn't.

A zombie horde poured from the parking garage near Angie, and she backed into the other lane, ignoring the cars and yelling drivers, still invoking her spell. She'd tossed her coffee and briefcase away and reached one hand toward the sky, pointing at the horde with the other.

Dru finished her rune set and barked her power word, then flung it down the street, its power crackling and setting Leery's fur on end as it raced past. Car alarms and horns marked its passage.

Behind Angie, a bugge and a long-legged, spindly-armed creature stepped out of the alley. The vittra had a long, hooked nose and what appeared to be bark the color of fall leaves for skin. Unaware, Angie backed straight toward them, trying to keep space between her and the zombies.

"Angie!" Dru cried, pointing at the unseelies, but Angie neither saw nor heard.

Leery heard her though, and he leaped atop the car next to him, then used the cars as stepping-stones to cross the river of traffic. He howled as he ran, leaping like a ballet dancer from car to car, his yellow eyes blazing at the unseelie assassins.

The vittra darted a glance at Leery and recoiled a step, but the bugge withdrew a huge nickel-plated pistol and leveled it at Angie's back.

Leery whined at Angie, but her attention was glued to the zombie horde that charged out from the parking garage and spilled into the street. With a snarl, he hurled himself through the air at the bugge, becoming a snarling fur-covered missile with flashing teeth and claws. The ugly creature glanced at him at last, eyes widening, but settled into a Weaver stance and returned his attention to Angie's back. Leery crashed into him, hooking his arm around the bugge's throat and whipping the unseelie around in a staggering semicircle with his momentum.

The report of the giant pistol crashed in Leery's ears, and he whined at the pain. The bugge thrashed and kicked, trying to regain his feet, and Leery went after his gun arm, sinking his claws into the creature's lean, lanky bicep.

Angie threw a glance over her shoulder, and the zombie horde screamed in unison, charging off the sidewalk and through the gaps in the traffic at her. But she jerked her skyward hand toward the horde, and power crackled from the heavens, blue-white bolts of electricity raining down on them, flinging undead bodies in every direction. Carmichael snapped her attention to the remaining zombies and began working another spell.

The bugge lost his grip on the pistol and turned on Leery, snarling and showing a mouthful of short, pointed teeth. Oriscoe peeled his lips back in a werewolf grin, showing every one of his own fangs, and growled deep in his chest. He kicked at the bugge's knee and wrinkled his nose at the green-wood snapping sound of the bugge's leg breaking.

He released the bugge's bicep as the creature fell into a screaming heap on the sidewalk, dragging Leery down with him. Something brown skittered past them and darted into the maze of cars. Oriscoe leaped to his feet, kicking the nickel-plated revolver into the storm drain as he did so. He threw back his head and howled a warning, then leaped to the roof of the nearest car, scanning the warren of spaces between the cars stalled in the traffic on 125th Street.

Dru trotted up the sidewalk on the same side as the zombie horde, drawing runes in the air and chanting in the *Verba Patiendi*. Angie had her eyes squeezed shut in concentration, one hand throwing gestures that looked like gang signs at the zombies, her other hand flung above her head, clawing at the swirl of dark clouds high above her head.

Leery shifted his gaze from place to place, scanning for anything brown and spindly for a moment, then charged toward Angie, stopping on the roof of the Yellow Cab to her left. He spun and tried to watch her back.

Angie shrieked a string of power words and gouts of vermillion flame with an eighteen-inch girth leaped skyward. Zombies close to the pillars of flame smoldered and smoked, and the odor of grilling meat filled the air. She glanced up at Leery and flashed him a smile that was one part victorious and two parts enraged. He nodded at her, and she turned back to the fight.

Dru stopped twenty yards from the zombies and hurled a spell into the back of them. It hit them like an invisible bulldozer, flinging broken bodies to the left and right with a sickening, dry-tinder crunch. She started another rune set, sketching in the air with a quick but sure hand.

Leery turned his attention back to the sea of automobiles, wrinkling his nose at the disgusting scent of all that exhaust. From the corner of his eye, he glimpsed something low to the ground streak from one car to the next, and he snapped his head in that direction, muscles tensed for another leaping tackle.

The three remaining zombies turned and ran up the street, away from Dru, and away from Angie's fire and lightning. Leery ignored them.

A low moaning—like the sound of building gale winds—started somewhere in the sea of cars, and Leery's lupine ears twitched toward the sound. A blast of cold air washed over him, ruffling his fur and sending a shiver racing down his spine. He put his nose in the air and sniffed, trying to make sense of the scents on that evil wind, despite the interference of the exhaust fumes.

The wailing moan rose in fervor, and the temperature dropped again. Leery threw a glance at Angie and nodded toward Dru. Angie shook her head at first, but when Leery nodded toward his partner again, Angie shrugged and began to back toward her.

The low moaning sound grew to a banshee wail, though no strong gust of wind accompanied it. The temperature continued to plummet, and static electricity charged the air. Angie's eyes opened wide and darted to something behind Leery. He whirled on the balls of his feet, his tail held straight out behind him.

"Leery! Look out!" shouted Angie. Immediately, she began chanting words in the *Verba Patiendi*, calling dark powers to her side.

Something the color of roasted coffee beans blurred toward him. It was the size of a Great Dane, and it rocketed forward, low to the ground—below the level of the passenger windows of the cars surrounding them. He couldn't get a clear picture of what the thing was, only that it was *wrong*. Oriscoe inhaled through his nose, then sneezed and shook his head at the god-awful fetor coming off the charging thing. He squatted low on the roof of the cab and sprang at the beast, arms out, claws extended. The dark thing jerked left, then right, zigzagging in the narrow aisle between the vehicles, a solid, metallic thunk accompanying each radical change in direction.

Pushing off the cars? What the hell is that thing? A growl rumbled in his throat as if in answer, and he could feel the raw, animalistic fury in his darker half at the oncoming beast's wrongness.

The creature came right at him, smelling wrong, looking wrong, moving wrong. It stank of burnt hair, spoiled meat, rotten produce, and coppery arterial blood. It made a noise as it rushed forward, a basso keen that set Leery's teeth on edge.

His skin tingled as another ward settled across him, but he didn't take his eyes off the wrongness coming ever closer. A mere ten steps separated them, but he still couldn't pick out visual details—as if it wore a cloak of velvet midnight shadows though it was only late afternoon.

Leery sank into a crouch, lowering his center of gravity in case the thing sprang at him. The creature banged off the rear quarter panel of the car to Leery's left and rocketed through the passenger-side window of the Yellow Cab to his right. The cabbie shrieked, but his cries didn't last more than a heartbeat before they were cut off with a sickening butcher-block sound and the driver-side window shattered outward.

Oriscoe howled a warning at Angie and dove across the yellow hood, his claws scoring the paint. The thing careened off a car in the opposing lane, then bee-lined it for the ALM. Scrambling for purchase, Leery inflicted more deep scratches in the cab's hood, but by the look of the blood splatter, the cabbie was past minding.

His wolf side was wrapped up in the chase, instinct trumping Leery's reason. He dove to the macadam, sprinting on all fours—his best possible speed. He snarled and barked as he ran, then gave in to the instinct to howl, to call his brethren to the hunt.

Three steps from Angie, the thing hurled itself up on its hind legs and slammed into her, wrapping its front limbs around her in a bear hug, then slamming her on her back, slashing at her with a pair of clawed hands that appeared from the black mist surrounding the thing. Her breath whoofed out of her, and she lost the spell she'd tried to cast. For a heartbeat, black magic swirled around them like a swarm of buzzing flies, then dissipated with a pop.

Fifteen steps away, Dru climbed onto the hood of a parked car. A set of runes glowed in the air to either side of her—one glowing in a fierce electric blue, the other a burning salamander orange. She pointed at the creature on top of Angie and whispered a word. The word echoed up and down the street as though she'd screamed it into a public address system, and the sound of it made Leery's skin creep and crawl.

The orange ward brightened and kept brightening until Leery thought he might go blind from its brilliance. Then Dru hurled it at the thing crouching over Angie, and it streaked forward like a bolt of lightning. It crackled as it struck the creature, outlining it with incandescent orange. The spell flared one final time, then burst apart.

But it took the creature's cloak of shadows with it.

The thing was covered in flat brown scales that looked like seed pods from a pinecone. It had six short limbs that ended in three clawed fingers, and a short nub of a tail. Small bumps on its skull defined its ears, and for eyes it had two large black orbs in front, and two smaller black orbs on either side of its head. Its mouth opened too wide for the size of its skull—more like the mouth of a crocodile than any dog. Viscous fluid dripped from its maw and sizzled where it touched the asphalt.

A yowie. I'll be damned, Leery thought right before he smashed into it at top speed, bowling the thing head over heels in a mass of snapping jaws and shredding talons. His momentum carried them into the front bumper of an SUV, knocking the vehicle catty-corner into the cab next to it.

Dru shouted a single word of power, and electric blue light surrounded Oriscoe. Strength surged through him, his muscles swelling with it, and his senses exploded as time seemed to slow.

The thing beneath him tilted its head to the side and snapped its powerful jaws. Leery jerked his head up and away, then drove forward, his own jaws open wide, his arms and legs pinning the thing against the SUV. He snapped his jaws shut around the thing's neck and locked them closed, growling and snarling the whole time. The six-legged creature thrashed, scouring Leery's side and belly with its claws, a strange mewling sound rumbling in its chest. Leery tightened his bite, bearing down with all the strength he could muster.

Foul black blood gushed into his mouth, bringing with it the taste of charred meat, mold, and flint. The creature became frantic, slashing at Oriscoe's flesh and jerking itself to and fro. Wherever it slashed him, the wounds burned and stung. *Poisoned claws*, he thought. *Neat trick.*

Leery snapped his head side to side, wrenching the creature's head left and right.

His vision glowed in the same shade of blue as Dru's spell, but it grew a shade less luminous with each expenditure of energy.

He wrenched the creature over and pinned it to the ground, digging his claws into the macadam for added leverage. The thing's struggles grew weaker and weaker as more and more black blood sprayed into Leery's mouth and dribbled from his jaws.

"Leery!" shouted Dru. "Angie's hurt!"

Leery growled at the thing dying under him, gave it a savage shake, and then let it go. It lay there in a heap, the twitching of one clawed foot growing more and more feeble as the thing's flesh slid and changed, its bulk and size melting away, leaving a bark-skinned, long-legged, spindly-armed creature with a hooked nose lying in the street. He sneezed to clear the vittra's foul blood from his mouth and its scent from his nose, then whirled and ran back to where Angie had fallen. Her eyes and lips were pressed shut in an angry rictus of pain and suffering, and her coat was rent down the left side. Blood slipped from the tear to pool beneath her.

"Protect us! I have to work fast to stop the poison."

Leery whined and licked Angie's hand, then leaped to the roof of the compact car next to him. He spun in a circle, gaze darting to everything that moved, his taloned feet screeching against the metal roof, his warning snarl echoing into the coming evening. Armed men pelted toward them from the building that housed Angie's office, Sam McCoy trailing in their wake. Other than that, no one moved under his baleful glare.

Below, Dru painted rune set after rune set in the air, endowed them with power, and cast them on Angie. Leery turned his gaze to McCoy, locked eyes with him, and howled, urging him to hurry.

16

Leery buttoned up one of Sam McCoy's spare shirts, then tucked it into a pair of Sam's jeans. Sam sat behind his desk, chair turned so he could stare out the window. "They'll fix her right up, Sam. Don't worry."

Sam shook his head and spoke without turning. "That was too close, Leery. A zombie horde and unseelie hit team? If you two hadn't given her a ride home, she'd have died in the street."

"But we did give her a ride, and she didn't die, Sam."

He whirled around in his chair, then, eyes blazing. "You know who's behind this."

"Mama Rose Marie."

"Damn right. She wants us to know she can get to any of us. That she can run things from inside our dungeon just as well as she could from outside."

"Then let's drop her down a well and brick it over. See how well she can run things from there. I'm not scared of the Zombie mafia, and neither is Angie. She kicked ass down there."

"Of course she did. But I want to know how Rose Marie Van Dee is getting orders out to her crew."

"Visitors? Phone calls?"

"She's been held *incommunicado* since her arrest."

Leery pursed his lips. "Maybe she gave the orders earlier."

"Maybe," said Sam in a distracted voice. "But maybe someone else is carrying her orders out."

"A guard?"

"No." Sam leaned forward and grabbed a pad of legal paper and began writing. "I'll get the warrants signed, but I want you to get set up on these phone numbers. Twenty-four-hour monitoring and recording, Leery. Trap and trace. The whole works."

"I love it when you get out the big guns. Who do these numbers belong to?"

Sam tore the sheet of the pad and held it out. "Paul Leibman."

Leery whistled and reached for the papers.

17

Angie groaned and readjusted her position in the hospital bed. "Help me get dressed."

"Lie back," said Dru in a firm voice. "You aren't going anywhere."

"But with Dee Terry and Jack Barnett missing, Sam needs—"

"Sam will get along without you for a day or so." Nogan turned cool eyes on McCoy and cocked her head to the side. "And if the Zombie mafia abducted them, Terry and Barnett are probably already spread all over New Jersey."

"Detective Nogan is right, Angie. You rest. I've got everything under control. I've got a call in to the Covenancy Marshals. We'll get it sorted out."

"Van Dee doesn't get to win, Sam! Not like this! I'm getting out of here, and I'm—"

"No." Dru put her palm on Angie's shoulder and pushed her back down. She bent close and whispered in Angie's ear. "I heard you invoke my mother back there. She would never forgive me if I allowed you to go and you got hurt."

Angie's eyes were wide as Nogan drew back.

"I take it that's settled, now?" asked Sam.

"It is," said Dru. "Isn't it, Angie?"

Angie could only nod.

18

At nine the next morning, Sam sat alone at the prosecutor's table. Fury still pounded in his veins with every beat of his heart, and truth be told, he'd kept the fire stoked. He turned and glanced at the doors leading to the hall. Leery was late.

Thoridn entered from the back of the courtroom, carrying his halberd, grim-faced. Though his gaze sailed past, Sam thought the bailiff knew what the plan for the morning was. He doubted Grimhildr Gyuki kept much from him. The *dvergr* glanced at the clock, then turned his gaze on Sam, one thick eyebrow lifted.

Leery entered from the hall and stood behind Sam at the bar. When Sam looked back, Oriscoe flashed a victorious smile. Sam turned back to Thoridn and nodded.

"All rise! Order, order! I call this court to order, the Just and Honorable Grimhildr Gyuki presiding."

Grimhildr swept in from her chamber doors, her black silk robe fluttering behind her like the wings of a Valkyrie. Her pale blue eyes shimmered with fury as she climbed to the bench, snatched up her gavel, and banged it on the sound block. She slumped into her seat and threw a searing glance at the defense table. "It is my understanding that an officer of my court was assaulted—nay, that murder was attempted on one of my officers this evening past."

Sam got to his feet. "That is correct, Your Honor. It was sheer providence that Detectives Oriscoe and Nogan were close enough to assist. Otherwise, I fear Ms. Carmichael would have been killed."

"Is it so?" Gyuki asked in a voice that sang of frigid, ice-filled plains scoured by strong arctic winds. Her eyes never left the defense table. "Imagine that. I have a case involving the Zombie mafia, the Unseelie Court, and a smattering of trolls from the land of my birth, and one of the court's officers is attacked by a zombie horde and two unseelie assassins." She threw a glance at Thoridn. "I wonder how that could have happened, Thoridn."

"I wouldn't know, Your Grace. But at least the trolls had enough sense to stay out of it. They wouldn't risk your wrath."

"Indeed. Mr. Leibman? Any guesses how it happened?"

"No, Your Honor, and I resent—"

"Mr. McCoy? Can you enlighten us?"

"I can, Judge Gyuki, though it pains me to do so."

"Indeed?" She arched one delicate eyebrow at him.

"Yes, Your Honor. I've known Paul Leibman these many years, and I'd have never guessed he could stoop so low."

"What is this?" asked Leibman. "I'll not be accused—"

"We have audio, Paul," said Sam in a quiet voice, but one that shook with fury. "So we know all about the follow-up attempt you ordered. That hospital is crawling with Claws and Warders, and raids were executed on your soldiers this morning. We have them all."

"*My* soldiers, Sam? I'm a magister. I think you are confusing me with my clients."

"Enough!" yelled Grimhildr. Thoridn stepped forward, knuckles white on the haft of his halberd. "I'll not have you continue to lie with impunity, Leibman. Arrest him, Detective Oriscoe."

"My pleasure, Your Honor." Leery swept through the swinging gates of the bar and grabbed Leibman's arms, wrenching them behind him, and cuffing his wrists. "Paul Leibman, you are under arrest. You have the right to remain silent, and to Ward from psychic interrogation. Anything you say, or think during unwarded conversation, can be used against you in a magister's court. You have the right to representation by a magister of your choosing. If you cannot afford a magister, one will be provided at no cost to you. Do you understand these rights as I've explained them?"

Leibman stood stunned, mouth opening and closing, but making no sound.

"Counselor, that's the smartest thing I've heard you say," said Leery. He turned his gaze to Judge Gyuki. "With your permission, Your Honor?"

"Get him out of my courtroom, detective."

"With pleasure, Judge." Holding Leibman right above the magister's elbow, he tugged him from behind the defense table and led him through the door to the holding cells.

Rose Marie Van Dee stood and cocked her head to the side. "This means a mistrial, right?" A small grin tugged at her lips.

Grimhildr narrowed her eyelids and compressed her lips into a tight, white line. "No, Ms. Van Dee, I don't think so. Instead, I'll have the Supernatural Defenders office assign someone to your case. The Court stands adjourned until next Monday. That will give your magister time to prepare."

"But what about me? Do you mean to tell me I'm to spend my days stuck in that filthy pit again? I'll not have it, Gyuki!"

Thoridn snapped his halberd up and down twice, the butt of the ancient weapon thundering on the hardwood floors. "*Judge Gyuki!*" he bellowed.

Rose Marie Van Dee spared him a single glance filled with fire and brimstone, then turned her attention back to Grimhildr. "This isn't *fair*! My magister committed those crimes on his own! *I had nothing to do with it*!"

Grimhildr chuckled. "Oh, I doubt that, *truykr*." She picked up her gavel and rapped it twice on the sound block. "Thoridn, dear, please secure the prisoner."

Wearing a savage grin, the *dvergr* advanced toward Rose Marie Van Dee, shifting his halberd diagonally across his body. She backed away from him, and he herded her toward the door to the holding cells.

Gyuki looked to the prosecution table and nodded at Sam. "See to it this mess goes away, Mr. McCoy."

"I will, Your Honor. I think Leibman, at least, will want to deal. Once he does, the troll or *Shuten-doji* or both will follow. We'll get Rose Marie Van Dee through their testimony."

CHAPTER 4

THE VERDICT

I

Paul Leibman sat slumped in the hardbacked wooden chair. His gaze roamed the floor at his feet, never straying more than a foot in any direction. The guards had taken his tie, belt, and shoelaces. His hair stood in disarray, as if he'd pulled at it, yanked tufts out.

"Why, Paul?" asked Sam in a quiet voice. "Why did you throw it all away?"

Leibman's head twitched, but his gaze didn't lift from the floor. He sucked in a long, unsteady breath and let it whistle out his nose. He slumped forward, resting his elbows on his knees and cradling his face in his hands. "I... I love her, Sam."

Sam shook his head.

"She's not what you think, Sam. She's lovely. Gentle and kind."

"No, she isn't, Paul. She's the head of a murderous bunch of savages and orders death and mayhem the way the rest of us might order lunch."

Leibman lifted his face and stared at McCoy. "That's true, but that's not *all* she is. She's also gentle and kind to her friends. To her lovers."

"Is that how she turned you, Paul? Sex?"

Leibman shook his head, his expression one of infinite weariness. "No, she doesn't know how I feel about her. She never made a single advance."

Sam lifted his hands and let them drop back to his side. "Then what, Paul? Your love is unrequited, yet for that, you threw away your entire life?"

Leibman swept a hand over his eyes, then up to smooth his wild hair. "You must think me a fool."

"I'll admit the thought has crossed my mind." Sam pulled out a chair and sat next to Leibman. "There's a way you can make this… Well, nothing can make this *right*, but there's a way you can begin making amends."

"I know, I know." Leibman spoke in the ghost of his courtroom voice, thin and weak. "But I can't do it, Sam. I can't betray her."

Sam reached into his briefcase and withdrew a small digital recorder. "No? Maybe this will change your mind." He pressed the play button.

"*I want a deal,*" said Rose Marie's voice in the recording. "*That dumb bastard has screwed everything up.*"

"*Why would I give you a deal, Ms. Van Dee? I've got you dead to rights. No wiggle room.*"

"*Hear her out, Mr. McCoy.*"

"She turned the Supernatural Defender away. That's Sig Shatenstein's voice you're hearing," said McCoy.

"*It's your nickel,*" said McCoy in the recording.

"*That...that* weasel *did those things without my knowledge. I've never done the things you told the jury I did. I've never bribed or threatened a juror, magister, judge, or anyone. It was all that fool, Leibman!*"

"*She's willing to testify to that, McCoy.*"

"*It would take more than her testimony, as you well know. What* proof *do you have?*"

"*I bugged my underling's phones. I have recordings of Leibman giving orders across a number of cases. Orders I knew nothing about.*"

"*Uh-huh,*" said McCoy.

"*I've also got records. Bank records showing Leibman funded the bribes, the zombie hordes, the assassins. He's the true head of the so-called Van Dee Cabal. I let him run things while I turned my mind to more pleasant pursuits.*"

"*Right.*"

"*I'm serious, Mr. McCoy. Paul Leibman is the one you should be prosecuting—*"

"Turn it off," whispered Leibman. "Sam, turn it off."

McCoy picked up the recorder and pressed the stop button. "You see, Paul?"

Leibman dropped his face to his hands, and his shoulders shook for a moment. "What can you do for me, Sam?"

"Testify against her, Paul, and I'll get you a reduced sentence. You'll spend twenty-five years in the dungeon of your choice—provided it's within the borders of this locus—in protective custody."

A sigh whistled from behind Leibman's hands. "And Rose Marie?"

"I'll bury her deep, Paul. She'll be lucky to see the sun in eighty years."

He drew a shaking breath and nodded. "Okay. Set it up."

2

Oriscoe pushed Angie's wheelchair into the gallery and wheeled her up to the swinging gates of the bar. Dru held the gates open, and Leery maneuvered her chair behind the prosecution table next to the smiling Sam McCoy. Angie sent a murderous stare Rose Marie Van Dee's way, but the zombie kept her gaze down.

Thoridn thumped the butt of his halberd on the floor. "All rise! Order, order! I call this court to order, the Just and Honorable Grimhildr Gyuki presiding."

The judge came gliding in from her chambers, wearing a bright smile. She mounted the steps to the bench and took up her gavel. She thumped it on the sound block and took her seat. "Be seated," she said. "I understand we've reached an accommodation, Mr. Shatenstein?"

The magister for the defense stood and cleared his throat. "We have, Your Honor."

"Good. Let's finish it, then."

"Yes, Your Honor." He lay his hand on Van Dee's shoulder, and she shrugged it off with an angry jerk. "You must," he whispered.

Shaking her head, Mama Rose Marie stood.

"Rose Marie Van Dee, you've entered a plea of guilty to one count each of the following charges: conspiracy to commit murder for hire, sale of body parts without a license, harvesting body parts without a license, intimidation of a law enforcement official, perverting the course of justice, improper action, and attempted murder of a law enforcement officer. Do you understand that your plea dispenses with a trial by a jury of your peers and equates to convictions by said juries for the charges I read?"

"Yes!" snapped Van Dee.

"Does the prosecution wish to hear an allocution?"

"Your Honor, I fear we'd all perish before Ms. Van Dee could complete a full allocution of her crimes. It will suffice for the defended to admit guilt to each of the charges."

"Very well," said Gyuki. She turned her piercing blue eyes back toward Van Dee. "The defendant will do as the prosecutor says."

Van Dee scoffed and scowled but admitted her guilt.

"Mr. McCoy?" asked Gyuki.

"The People are satisfied, Your Honor."

"Very well. Rose Marie Van Dee, I accept your plea and find you guilty of all charges. In accordance with your plea agreement, I sentence you to four lifetimes in a dungeon to be determined by the Locus of New York's Department of Correction. Sentences are to be served *consecutively* and without the possibility of parole or early release."

"Your Honor!" shouted Shatenstein. "Our agreement calls for leniency."

Grimhildr's smile could have flash-frozen falling rain. "That is leniency, Mr. Shatenstein. If I had my way, your client would even now be stepping up to the stake, awaiting ignition." She rapped her gavel. "Court adjourned."

<u>CHAPTER 5</u>

THE END

I

Van Dee's screams could be heard out in the hall, and the sound of it put a smile on all four of their faces. Angie was pale, and exhaustion lined her face, but her eyes twinkled with glee. "How long do you think it will be before she fires Shatenstein and has a new magister papering us with appeals?"

Sam shrugged. "I imagine it's already in the works."

"Too bad about Leibman," said Angie.

"He made his own choices," said Sam. "And twenty-five years is a gift. He owes you big time."

"He—" Angie bit off her words as six men in Covenancy Marshal windbreakers came in from the front steps. "What do they want?"

Sam scowled. "I don't know."

The six men walked toward them, led by the tall black man who'd picked up Dee Terry and Jack Barnett. They stopped as they drew closer, and the tall man pulled a blue-backed writ from his inner coat pocket. He held it out to Sam, his face as impassive as that of a marble bust.

"Where's the coffee?" Leery asked. "You should always bring coffee—it's the polite thing to do."

The ebony-skinned man sneered at Oriscoe and turned his gaze on McCoy, raising his eyebrows in a silent question.

"I admit I doubted you were really a Marshal until I saw that sneer. You're way too stuck up to be a hitman."

Other than a slight narrowing of his eyelids, the tall black man ignored Oriscoe.

Sam took the order, opened it, and scanned it before handing it to Angie. "I hope you're kidding. Witness protection? Van Dee is the one witnesses need protection *from!*"

The tall man shook his head. "You've had your bite of the apple, McCoy. Now, it's the Covenancy's turn. Van Dee will give us the heads of at least three other occult cabals."

"*She gets no time?*" hissed Angie. "We convicted her of *attempted murder of a law enforcement officer,* among other things!"

The marshal's eyes twitched toward Angie, but he never met her irate gaze. "She has information—"

"I could shoot him," said Oriscoe, and though his tone made it sound like a joke, his eyes were hard and cold. "Want me to shoot him? I don't mind."

"Who's behind this?" demanded Dru. "Give me a name." She pulled out her phone and flipped it open.

"Signed by a Covenancy judge," said the tall, solemn marshal. "There's nothing you can do."

"Want to bet on that?" snapped Dru. "Give me the name."

The marshal shook his head. "I'm here as a courtesy. This writ allows me to take custody of Rose Marie Van Dee, and I could have done that from holding without saying a word."

"Oh, well, gee, thanks for *nothing*," grated Angie. "You know she almost succeeded in killing me?"

The marshal's gaze twitched her direction, but again it didn't move far enough to meet her stare. "I don't make the decisions."

"Now I *really* want to shoot him," growled Leery.

"Right, of course you don't make any decisions. Your kind never do," said Dru. "Tell me who made *this* decision." Her thumb hovered over her phone, ready to speed-dial a contact named "Mom."

"This deal was cleared by both the Grand Cynosure and your Locus Cynosure."

Dru gave a curt nod as her thumb descended. She turned and walked a few steps away. "Hello? Mom?"

"Uh-oh. Someone's in trouble," Leery chanted in a singsong voice. "Before this is over, you'll wish you'd brought me coffee."

The marshal shot a cross look at him, then held his hand out for the writ. "We'll go get our prisoner, now." Angie dropped the writ to the ground next to her wheelchair, and the tall man stooped to pick it up. As he straightened, Angie's hand shot out and grabbed his arm. "Don't you treat her like a queen! She should suffer for all the pain she's caused in this Locus. Make her wait tables or clean toilets."

"What about the others?" Sam asked.

"What others?"

"Paul Leibman. *Shuten-doji*. The troll, Lothidn? The various unseelie involved in this sordid affair? Are their sentences to be reduced?"

The tall man shrugged. "The writ only mentions Rose Marie Van Dee. The others are yours to do with as you please."

"Where's the justice?" Angie murmured.

"It's not too late for me to shoot him," said Leery. "That would be a big step toward justice, if you ask me."

Dru rejoined them, wearing a tight smile. "My mother's going to make a few calls. Mr. McCoy, she asks that you do what you can to delay things."

McCoy nodded. "I think Judge Gyuki is still here." He snatched the writ from the marshal's hand and set off for the judge's chambers.

"Well, sport, you're in for a treat," said Leery, wearing a wide smile. "Too bad you didn't bring the judge coffee, either. She loves it."

2

Grimhildr scanned the writ, her eyes narrowing with each line. When she finished, she looked up at Sam, and simply said, "No."

"I feel the same way, Your Honor. You can imagine how Angie must feel."

"Where are these marshals?"

Sam hooked his thumb over his shoulder. "I left them in the hall outside your courtroom."

"Come with me," she said. She went out into the courtroom, her strides long and full of purpose and fury. "Thoridn!" she called.

"My liege?" He came bustling in from the clerk's chambers.

"Bring your halberd."

"Yes, Your Grace." He reached behind him and pulled the runed halberd out of thin air. He set his face in grim lines, his eyes boring into Sam's.

"It's not me," Sam said and turned to follow the judge.

The three of them stepped out into the hall. Grimhildr bowed her head toward Dru. "Your Grace," she said with a sunny smile. "I bid you welcome. Many blessings to Her Majesty, your royal mother."

Dru nodded her head. "I will convey them to her. She asks for a few moments to confer with...others."

The judge turned her gaze to the marshals, and as she did, the warmth drained from her face. "I've read your writ. You may not have my prisoner."

"But..." The tall man shook his head and looked at his comrades. "We have a writ."

"Yes. I'm quashing your writ."

"You can't do that."

Thoridn growled into his beard.

"Oh, I misunderstood," said Grimhildr. "I thought I was the judge, and you were the visitor. My apologies." Her tone dripped with sugar.

"I mean that you can't quash a Covenancy writ. You're a Locus judge."

"Oh, is that how it works?" She turned to her bailiff. "Thoridn, please go to the holding cells and ensure no one breaks my order of isolation for prisoner Van Dee."

He snapped a salute, and his gaze snapped to Leery's and held there until Oriscoe nodded. Satisfied Grimhildr would be safe, he jogged away to do as she bid him.

"I'm just doing my job," said the tall marshal. "I have no say in this."

"No, you do not," said Grimhildr. "But *I* do, and I say you wait for the Witch Queen's pleasure."

Dru grimaced but kept her head up, her back straight.

"It's okay," whispered Angie. "Sam already knew."

Dru shot a glance at Leery.

"No," said Sam. "Oriscoe kept your secret. I found out another way."

She shrugged her shoulders. "It was bound to come out."

The marshal's phone trilled, and he fished it out of his inner coat pocket, stepping away and grimacing at the caller ID. He murmured into the phone for a moment, then hung up. "Come on," he said to the other marshals, ignoring everyone else. "The Grand Cynosure has changed his mind."

"Bye," said Leery. "Don't be strangers. Only next time? Bring coffee."

I hope you've enjoyed this episode of CLAW & WARDER and are chomping at the bit to get on to the next. *Mitzvah: CLAW & WARDER Episode 3* can be found here: https://ehv4.us/4cw3.

If you've enjoyed this novel, please consider joining my Readers Group by visiting https://ehv4.us/join. Or follow me on BookBub by visiting my profile page there: https://ehv4.us/bbub.

For my complete bibliography, please visit: https://ehv4.us/bib.

Books these days succeed or fail based on the strength of their reviews. I hope you will consider leaving a review—as an independent author, I could use your help. It's easy (I promise). You can leave your review by clicking on this link: https://ehv4.us/2revcw2.

AUTHOR'S NOTE

I hope you are enjoying these books—the Witch Queen knows I am. And to be honest, that comes as a bit of a surprise. I'd never considered writing Urban Fantasy (though many have told me my other dark fiction books are at least kissing cousins to the genre), and I have been pleasantly surprised by how much I look forward to writing about Leery and Dru every day.

It's funny where life takes us sometimes, and some of my life's destinations have left a little to be desired. I'm happy to say the journey the CLAW & WARDER series is taking me on has been a fun one, and one I hope to continue for a long time.

Don't get me wrong: I'm still getting my daily dose of horror (writing a long horror novel at the same time as writing these first few CLAW & WARDER books) and have ideas for both a post-apocalyptic epic and another dark fantasy tale. Plus, more ideas for horror novels than I can shake a crucifix at.

I'm glad you're here with me, and I hope you're having as much fun as I am. Please don't hesitate to drop by my Facebook page located at https://fb.me/erikhenryvick or my Readers' Group at https://ehv4.us/fbog and say hello!

ABOUT THE

AUTHOR

Erik Henry Vick is an author who happens to be disabled by an autoimmune disease (also known as his Personal Monster™). He writes to hang on to the few remaining shreds of his sanity. His current favorite genres to write are dark fantasy and horror.

He lives in Western New York with his wife, Supergirl; their son; a Rottweiler named after a god of thunder; and two extremely psychotic cats. He fights his Personal Monster™ daily with humor, pain medicine, and funny T-shirts.

Erik has a B.A. in Psychology, an M.S.C.S., and a Ph.D. in Artificial Intelligence. He has worked as a criminal investigator for a state agency, a college professor, a C.T.O. for an international software company, and a video game developer.

He'd love to hear from you on social media:

Blog: https://erikhenryvick.com
Twitter: https://twitter.com/BerserkErik
Facebook: https://fb.me/erikhenryvick
Amazon author pages:
    USA: https://ehv4.us/amausa
    UK: https://ehv4.us/amauk
Goodreads Author Page: https://ehv4.us/gr
BookBub Author Profile: http://ehv4.us/bbub

Made in the USA
Middletown, DE
07 March 2023

26356023R00158